EMBA
OAK
AND THE
TERRIBLE
TOMORROWS

Emba Oak and the Terrible Tomorrows
An original concept by author Jenny Moore
© Jenny Moore, 2022

Cover artwork by David Dean
© David Dean, 2022

Published by MAVERICK ARTS PUBLISHING LTD
Studio 11, City Business Centre, 6 Brighton Road,
Horsham, West Sussex, RH13 5BB
+44 (0) 1403 256941
© Maverick Arts Publishing Limited October 2022

First edition October 2022

A CIP catalogue record for this book is available
at the British Library.

ISBN: 978-1-84886-893-9

EMBA OAK
AND THE
TERRIBLE TOMORROWS

JENNY MOORE

Other Maverick books by Jenny Moore:

Agent Starling: Operation Baked Beans

Audrey Orr and the Robot Rage

Bauble, Me and the Family Tree

The Misadventures of Nicholas Nabb

To my Team of Terrific Tomorrows:
Dafydd, Lucy and Dan xx

A hero forged in fiercest flame,
A child of iron and pain,
By blood shall heal and chasm seal
A kingdom torn in twain.

The Final Prophecy* from the Tome of
Terrible Tomorrows

*Also known as
Odolf's prophecy.
(But only by Odolf!)

(Almost) Chapter 1

The Nerve-Wracking Knock of Destiny

All the best stories and adventures start with a knock at the door. With a mysterious, shadowy stranger, or a blood-bathed warrior seeking shelter for the night. With a spell-bound hero, bringing danger and peril in their wake. First the knocking—the sharp rap of bony knuckles against waiting wood—and then the life-changing quest...

Yes, Emba Oak had listened to enough tantalising tales round the fire to know that *all* the best stories started with a knock at the door. And hers, it would seem, was no exception. Well, except for the door part. Emba didn't actually *have* a door.

(Actual)
Chapter 1

The Thrilling Thwump of Destiny

Emba Oak was scraping squirrel stew splashes off her tunic, when she heard a strange noise coming from outside the cave. *Thwump, thwump, thwump.*

She paused, ears straining in the eerie quiet that followed. It didn't sound like the sort of noise Fred would make. Fred wasn't a thwumping kind of woman. And it didn't sound like Odolf either. Besides, Odolf had scarpered straight back into the woods after dinner, as usual, to squeeze in some more hero-training before nightfall. For a scrawny runaway blacksmith's assistant, he was very big on hero-training.

Thwump, thwump, thwump. A quivery, shivery feeling snaked along Emba's spine as she swapped her tunic-scraping stone for her scaring-off one.

Whoever—or *what*ever—was out there, it was best to be prepared. She was still haunted by memories of the bewitched widower of Nether Mynd, who'd attacked her with his sharpened walking stick after mistaking her for a blood-sucking cave spirit. If it hadn't been for the thick, lizard-like scales on Emba's arms and legs, she'd have been in serious trouble. And now, as she held her breath and listened, Emba had the funniest, tingliest feeling that trouble had found her all over again…

Thwump, thwump, thwump.

It sounded like wet rope whipping against the slimy rock wall—only heavier and more *monstrous*. Emba had a fleeting vision of the eight-legged sea-monster from the front cover of the Tome of Terrible Tomorrows, but pushed the image away again. What would a sea-monster be doing in Witchingford Wood? Unless it had come to seek the Tome's advice… The ancient book of prophecies had an answer for everything, if you were wise enough to understand its riddles (which ruled out everyone except Fred).

Thwump, thwump, thwump.

Emba dropped down onto her stomach and wriggled through the narrow crawl hole that separated her and Fred's private living quarters from the main body of the cave. The noise reverberated through the stone walls to meet her, echoing round her skull. But no sooner had she reached the other side than the thwumping stopped again, with nothing but the answering thump of her own heart to fill the silence.

She ducked under a row of stalactites and squinted through the gathering gloom. It was an eerie, shifting gloom, that seemed to reach into the curves and corners of the cave and then ease itself back again. Almost as if the darkness was breathing...

Ridiculous, Emba told herself firmly. The seasons were on the turn, that was all. Dusk came quickly at this time of year and the cooking fire was all but out. It was her own silly fault for not bringing a lantern. She crept on towards the cave entrance, her scaring-off stone clenched tight inside her fist.

"Hello," she called, the strange tingling feeling growing stronger than ever. "Who's there?"

For a moment, there was nothing. No answer.

No sound. And then…

"*RRRROOOOOOOAAAAAAAARRRRRR,*" came a cave-shaking reply.

Emba flung herself back against the wall, eyes clamped shut in fear, her scaled knees trembling. *A bear!* she thought. A growling, snarling GIANT of a bear. Or a boar, like the one that had gouged Odolf's stomach with its tusks the year before. Emba could hear it snuffling and pawing at the ground as it edged closer… and closer…

Please, she begged, too terrified to move. *Please don't hurt me.*

"Rrruhh?" came a softer, more considered kind of roar. "Rrrhur-hurh?"

No, that didn't sound like a boar. Or a bear… and it didn't smell like one either. It smelt of mist and smoke, and a dark glittering rush of something deep and terrible and wonderful, all at the same time. It made the hairs on the back of Emba's neck tingle to attention and sent her stomach spinning.

Emba took a deep breath and opened one eye… and then rather wished she hadn't.

She was right. It wasn't a boar.

It wasn't a bear.

It was impossible—that's what it was.

She opened her other eye, to make doubly sure, and there it was.

A dragon.

Chapter 2

The Phantom Fire-breather

Yes, a dragon. Well, sort of…

From where Emba was standing, pressed against the cave wall on trembling legs, it looked like the dragon from her dreams—the huge, roaring fire-breather who came swooping into her sleeping mind each night, with a wild beating of its bone-threaded wings and a sharp flash of gleaming talons. But *that* dragon was solid and real (by dream standards anyway), while the snorting creature in front of her now was more air than flesh. A flickering, silvered echo of a dragon. A phantom. And, unlike the dragon in her dream, it hadn't scooped Emba up and carried her off into the clouds like a bird of prey with its latest catch. Not yet, anyway. *This* dragon stood staring back at her from the cave entrance, raising its enormous tail up in the air, only to bring it thumping back down against the rock floor. *Thwump, thwump, thwump.*

But that's impossible, Emba reminded herself. Dragons only existed in stories and dreams and idle imaginings while stirring a pot of squirrel stew. Everyone knew that. Everyone, it would seem, except for the roaring beast in front of her now.

"Rooooooaaahhhhhrrr!"

The impossible creature's cry thrilled through her like a physical shudder of fear. Or was it a shiver of excitement? It was terrifying and wondrous and bone-shakingly shiversome, all at the same time. But still utterly impossible. If it wasn't for the hard press of her scaring-off stone against her clenched fingers, and the sharpened jut of cave wall against her left shoulder, Emba might have wondered if she was dreaming even now. But in truth, she'd never felt more awake. More alive.

"H-h-hello," she said, staring up into the milky swirl of an enormous eye. "Are you looking for Winnifred? The Wise Hermit of Witchingford Wood?"

The dragon blinked.

"I… I'm afraid she's not here at the moment. She's g-gathering wortbane for one of her medicines…"

"I know," interrupted a familiar voice. Emba watched in horror as Odolf came striding into the cave, straight through the dragon's stomach and out the other side. "*She's* the one who told me to come and check on you," he said, as if nothing had happened. "She was worried you were in danger and wanted me to run on ahead and see."

Of course I'm in danger, thought Emba. *And so are you. Look!*

But Odolf seemed oblivious to the ghostly beast camped outside the cave. "I *told* her there was nothing to worry about, but you know what she's like. What's with all the fancy 'Wise Hermit' talk, anyway?" he added, straightening his stolen 'hero helmet', which had slipped down over his eyes. Odolf insisted on wearing it for his hero practice, despite the fact that it was three sizes too big for him. Despite the fact there was no mention of any helmet-wearing in the Final Prophecy—or 'his' prophecy as he liked to call it.

"What's wrong with plain old 'Fred'?" he demanded.

"I wasn't talking to *you*," said Emba, struggling to make sense of what she'd seen—what she was *still* seeing. "I was talking to the dragon."

Odolf let out an unheroic snort of laughter. "The *dragon?* Have you been dreaming again? Or is this like last week when you thought someone was watching you?"

"Of course it's not a dream," Emba snapped. "And for your information there *was* someone watching me last week. I could feel their eyes following me through the wood. Well, not *just* their eyes, obviously, I mean…"

"Rhhurr-hooooaahhhhh," interrupted the dragon, shaking its head from side to side as if it was trying to tell her something. "Rhhhurr, rhurr, raaarrr." And *still* Odolf didn't respond. Not so much as an eyelid flicker.

"Can't you see it?" asked Emba, pointing to the huge beast outside. "Can't you *hear* it?" But it was clear from the silly, teasing look on her friend's face that he couldn't. And neither could Fred, it seemed.

The old woman's long, gnarled toenails tap-tap-tapped against the cave floor as she came hobbling through the dragon after Odolf, a look of worry etched into her wrinkled face.

"Oh Emba, you're here!" she panted, clutching at her chest. Her left eye was twitching, wildly. "Thank goodness. I had a vision of a big crack in the sky as I was picking the wortbane. I was sure something *awful* had happened to you."

"Something awful? Like the arrival of an enormous dragon, you mean?" What was wrong with everyone? Why was Emba the only one who could see it?

Fred paled. "A dragon?" she repeated. "Why would you say that, dear?"

"BECAUSE IT'S STANDING RIGHT THERE!" A fiery darkness flared in Emba's belly, the words roaring out of her. The dragon roared back, its scaled body glistening as a golden column of flame burst from its mighty jaws. It was like a hundred cooking fires all rolled into one. The cave walls shimmered in the backblast of heat that came barrelling towards them, nearly knocking Emba off her feet. She could feel it inside her too, the same heat filling her chest, burning up inside her throat. But the others didn't even flinch. They were as oblivious to the creature's flames as they were to the creature itself.

Emba cowered against the rock, waiting for the dragon to turn its angry fire on her, reducing her to burnt bones and ash. But the dragon dropped down onto its belly instead, forcing its mighty snout in through the cave entrance towards her. Two milky eyes blinked. *A sad kind of blink*, thought Emba, although she couldn't say why.

"What do you want?" she asked, forcing the words out through trembling lips.

But the dragon didn't reply. Of course it didn't. Even dragons in stories couldn't *talk*. And yet Emba couldn't shake the feeling that it was trying to tell her something.

"I'm sorry," she whispered. "I don't understand."

The dragon shook its head—once, twice, three times—and turned to go, stretching out its enormous boned wings and taking to the sky like a giant bird. A ghostly four-legged bird with a long, swishing tail, steering through the air behind it. Emba watched as it thundered through the gloom, up, up, up towards a pulsing red crack in the sky. *That* was pretty impossible too. Since when did the sky have cracks in it? That must have been what Fred had seen in her vision.

"The dragon," Emba said, turning back to the others. "It's gone." She should have been relieved. She should have been *shaking* with relief. But she wasn't. She didn't know what she felt... other than hot. Little flames of dark heat were still dancing in her belly and chest, burning at the back of her throat.

"That's because it was never here in the first place," said Odolf. "The only dragon round here is the one on my belt buckle," he added, tracing his finger over the intricate iron beast threaded onto his leather belt.

"Hush now," said Fred, brushing him aside. "If Emba says she saw a dragon then that's what she saw. There are other worlds beyond the mortal realm, you know."

Odolf laughed. "Imaginary worlds, you mean? What's next? Ogres? Fairies?"

"I *did* see it," Emba insisted. "I could feel it too. My insides are still burning, even now." She turned to Fred. "And the crack in the sky. I saw that as well."

"*You're* the one who's cracked, if you ask me," said Odolf.

Fred glared at him. "Hush now, I said. That's enough out of you. Thank you for your help but I can take it from here. Perhaps you should get back to your training and leave me to talk to Emba. It's time she knew the truth."

Emba's eyes widened. "The truth? What do you mean?"

Fred took hold of Emba's hands and squeezed them tight. "*Your* truth, my dear. Who you really are. Let me fetch a cooling draught for your throat and I'll tell you everything."

Chapter 3

The Truth, The Whole Truth, and Nothing but the Truth—and Some Toenails

Odolf took off his hero helmet and added some fresh wood to the dwindling fire, stoking it with a long stick until it crackled back to life. The dying embers turned to orange tongues of flame.

"Hero-training can wait," he said, grinning to himself as he took a seat on the fur rug, draping Fred's goat hair blanket across his shoulders like a shawl. His eyebrow danced with excitement. Just the one eyebrow though. According to Odolf, the other one had been burnt away during his blacksmith training and never grew back. "This sounds too good to miss. Let me guess, it starts with a knock at the door? With a mysterious, shadowy stranger, or a blood-bathed warrior seeking shelter for the night... That's how *all* the best stories start."

Fred added a few drops of green tincture to a clay beaker of water. "Well this one doesn't," she said. "This one starts with an egg." She handed the beaker to Emba. "Drink up, dear. This will help with the burning."

Emba did as she was told, the cool mixture trickling down her throat like icy mountain stream water on a summer afternoon. The flaming feeling inside was as strong as ever, but she smiled back at Fred as if it was all better now. It wasn't an *unpleasant* feeling, she realised. It was just… just… Well, Emba didn't quite know *what* it was.

She joined Odolf on the rug by the fire and Fred took her usual seat on the hand-carved stool they'd made for her the previous winter, to save her 'old aching bones', as she liked to call them.

"Well now," said Fred, the furrowed lines of her face illuminated by the dancing flames. Her left eye twitched again. "I don't quite know where to begin."

"With the egg, of course," said Odolf. "If there's no door-knocking to start us off, then it must be the egg.

What kind of egg was it? A chicken? A partridge? A wren?"

"A dragon?" asked Emba, softly. The scales on her legs tingled and itched with anticipation, as if this was the answer she'd been waiting for all along. The answer to a question she'd never known to ask.

Fred shot her a strange sort of look, somewhere between surprise and worry. "Yes, Emba dear, that's right. It *was* a dragon's egg. At least, that's what I thought when I first found it, smouldering under the still-smoking embers of a burnt oak tree. It was a deep blue colour—blue as Dreamer's Pool—and as big as my head. What else could it have been?"

"An ogre moth chrysalis?" suggested Odolf. "*They're* blue."

Emba kicked him in the shin. "Shh, this is important." She could tell as much by the twitch in Fred's eye. It always twitched when she was worried.

"It was hot to the touch," Fred went on. "*Too* hot. It burnt my fingers when I tried to pick it up. But I couldn't just leave it there. If there *was* a dragon inside, then…"

"Then you should have run," said Odolf. "That's what *I'd* do if I found a dragon egg."

So much for you being the great hero from the Final Prophecy, thought Emba. *That doesn't sound very heroic to me.* But she bit her tongue and said nothing, willing Fred on with her story.

"So I waited to see if anyone—or any*thing*—was coming back for it," said the old lady. "I sat down and I waited. I waited and waited."

"And…?" said Odolf.

"And…?" said Emba.

"And waited," said Fred. She stared into the flickering flames, lost in her own thoughts.

"Perhaps we could skip over the waiting bit," Emba suggested. "What happened after that?"

"Nothing," said Fred. "So once it was finally cool enough to touch, I scooped it up in my skirts and carried it back here to the cave. Then I wrapped it in furs to keep it snug, and waited for it to hatch." Fred paused again, her left eye twitching harder than ever.

"And then?" coaxed Emba.

"I waited," said Fred. "I waited and waited…"

Odolf rolled his eyes and grinned, but Emba was too impatient to see the funny side.

"It *did* hatch in the end, though?" she asked. It wouldn't be much of a story otherwise.

Fred nodded. "Yes," she said. "I woke up one morning to find a big, jagged crack running across the shell... and a strange mewling sound coming from inside."

"Hm," said Odolf. "That doesn't sound much like an ogre moth."

Emba ignored him. There was something important coming—she could feel it.

"No, it wasn't an ogre moth," agreed Fred. "*Or* a dragon. It was a baby. A beautiful baby girl, with yellow-hazel eyes and glittering scales over her arms and legs."

Odolf gasped out loud. "But that's..." He turned from Fred to Emba. "That sounds like you."

Fred nodded again. "Yes, Odolf, that's right. It was Emba. My beautiful yellow-eyed hatchling." She reached over and squeezed Emba's elbow. "I knew you were special from the moment I saw you. And I made a vow to myself, there and then, to protect you with my life."

Emba scratched at her legs, raking her fingernails across the sudden itch and prickle of her scales. It felt like insects crawling under her skin. But that was nothing compared to the furious wriggle and squirm of thoughts inside her head. "You mean I'm... I'm not..." *Not human.* The end of the sentence caught in her throat, refusing to come out. She could hardly bring herself to *think* it. Because that really *was* impossible. And Emba Oak had already had her fill of impossible things for one day, thank you very much.

"You're no less human than we are," Fred assured her, reading her mind. "But maybe there's a bit of something extra in you too. Extra-special, that is."

Extra-weird, you mean, thought Emba, scratching furiously at her arms. She'd always known she was different—of course she had. None of the visitors to the cave had yellow eyes and scaled skin, and neither did the staring locals she passed in the woods or on her rare trips to the market with Fred. But now she was officially a freak. An impossibility. *People* didn't hatch out of eggs.

Tears welled in her yellow eyes. "Is that what the dragon was doing here?" she asked. "Has it come to take me back?" *Back where though?*

Fred shook her head. "Your guess is as good as mine, I'm afraid. All I know is that you're safe here with me. With us," she added, glancing across at Odolf, as if they were a team. But then they *were* a team, Emba realised. The dark-haired runaway felt like part of their family now. "We won't let anything happen to you, will we, Odolf?"

Odolf put his hero helmet back on and puffed out his chest. "Of course we won't. It'll take more than a pesky dragon to defeat Odolf Bravebuckle... Although fighting it might be tricky if I can't actually see it."

"I'm sure it won't come to that," said Fred, soothingly. "Whatever it wanted with Emba, I don't think it meant any harm."

"Or maybe my charm scared it off." Emba clutched the leather pouch dangling from her neck. The yellow eye embroidered onto the front was scarcely visible now beneath a thick accumulation of grease and grime. "Is that why you gave it to me?" she asked Fred. "In case the dragon came back for its missing egg? In case it came back and found *me?*"

Odolf snorted. "It'd take more than a bag of mouldy old toenails to scare off a dragon."

"Mouldy?" repeated Fred. "*Mouldy?* My toenails are the source of untold wisdom and power, I'll have you know. That's why I never cut them. It took me twenty-seven years to grow the one in that pouch— and a full day and a half to saw through it. But that was a sacrifice I was willing to make for my new charge. For my little Emba."

Emba traced her finger across the embroidered eye. She'd worn the pouch of magic toenail shards next to her heart for as long as she could remember. It felt as much a part of her now as her *own* toenails. As her own toes. What would happen if she took it off? Would the dragon come back?

The possibility sent hot chills down Emba's spine. Maybe there was a small, confused part of her that *wanted* the dragon to find her again. That wanted to know who she really was. And what if that small, confused part of her was right? What if it was time she stopped hiding and faced the truth? She fingered the leather cord round her neck, daring herself to lift it off over her head.

Fred must have read her mind. "But it's not to protect you from dragons," she said quickly, reaching out to stop her. "It's to keep you hidden from Necromalcolm."

"Necrowho?" asked Emba, letting go of the cord with a start. "What are you talking about?"

"Necromalcolm," Fred said again. "He's a wicked necromancer who's obsessed with dragons and flight. The Tome of Terrible Tomorrows showed me a prophecy about him not long after I found you:

"His dragon lust shall never lie," she intoned, reciting the words by heart,

"Until he claims both Earth and Sky,
And men shall fall and men shall die
Before the greed of one who'd fly.
Beware his scrying eye of truth,
Beware the bowl that sees,
No walls can stop its fearsome gaze,
No doors, no locks, no keys.

At least, I *think* the prophecy's about him," Fred added. "He was pretty famous within the magic community, back before you were born. One of the most powerful dark magicians in the land, according to my research, with legions of spirits at his command."

Before I hatched, you mean, thought Emba, still struggling to come to terms with the idea.

"What about the 'beware the bowl' part?" Odolf pulled a face. "That doesn't sound very scary to me."

"You'd be surprised," said Fred. "In the hands of someone like Necromalcolm, a scrying bowl can be a powerful weapon. It allows him to see things happening on the other side of the world. It helps him keep track of his enemies and search out his victims."

"Like a magic porridge bowl, you mean?" asked Odolf.

Fred smiled. "Not exactly, no... more like a shimmering basin of water that shows you the answers to your questions. A bit like the Pool of Perilous Perception, I suppose."

The pool of what now? thought Emba.

But Odolf seemed to know exactly what Fred

meant. "Oh, I see," he said. "So I could ask this bowl thing whose goat ate my undergarments while I was washing in the river last week and it would show me?" He thought for a moment. "But what's this bowl magician got to do with Emba?" he asked. "Why does she need protecting from *him?*"

"Like I said, Necromalcolm's obsessed with harnessing the power of flight," explained Fred. "And for that he needs dragon blood. But there *are* no dragons anymore. Not since the gap between our realm and theirs was sealed."

"Which just leaves *me*," said Emba quietly. "If he thinks there's dragon blood in *my* veins, he…"

Fred nodded. "Exactly. But as long as you keep wearing your magic pouch, his scrying bowl won't be able to find you. You'll be perfectly safe."

"But… but…" Emba was thinking about that time in the woods a few weeks ago, when she was playing tree-chase with Odolf. She was remembering how her pouch had caught on a hog chestnut branch as she scrambled after him, snapping the leather thong in two. It had been easy enough to fix once she realised what had happened... once she'd finally noticed it was missing and retraced her steps to find it. But what if this Necromalcolm happened to be looking in his bowl while she'd left herself unprotected?

"Hush now," said Fred. "That's why I didn't tell you any of this before. I didn't want you to worry. The chances of Necromalcolm tracking you down without his scrying bowl are tiny. He'd have to scour the whole country. The whole world. Besides, no one has heard of him in years. I don't even know if he's still alive."

"But the prophecy..." said Emba.

"You let *me* take care of that," Fred told her. "That's my job."

"So if someone *was* to come looking for a girl with dragon scales..." began Odolf. His suntanned face looked strangely pale all of a sudden. "If a strange man in the woods, let's say, started asking questions about where he might find someone matching Emba's description..."

"You'd deny everything," said Fred firmly. "Tell him you'd never seen anyone like that round here."

Odolf looked paler than ever. "Ah," he said. "Oh dear. I think it might be a little late for that."

Chapter 4

The Not-So-Wise Hero of Witchingford Wood

"What do you mean, it might be a little late for that?" demanded Fred. Her left eye was twitching like crazy now. "Who have you been talking to?"

"Just a man," said Odolf, picking at the fur rug with his fingers. "A man I met in the woods."

"What kind of man? What did he look like?"

Odolf shrugged. "He didn't look like a necromancer, if that's what you mean." He paused. "What *is* a necromancer, anyway?"

"An evil sorcerer," said Fred, "who communes with dead spirits for the purposes of black magic."

Emba shivered, despite the heat of the fire and the burning feeling in her chest.

"He had a beard, I think, if that helps?" added Odolf

after a moment's consideration.

"Not really, no," said Fred. "Every man over the age of twenty has a beard. But you said he was asking questions... what sort of questions?"

"He asked if I'd seen any dragon girls nearby. And then he said something about a vision his master had seen...and something about spirits..." Odolf cast a nervous glance at Emba. "Oh dear. That does sound a *bit* like a necromancer now I think about it. Or rather his *master* sounds a bit like one."

"And what did you tell him?" interrupted Fred. "Come on, think, Odolf. This is important."

Emba's stomach tightened as she held her breath, waiting for the answer.

"I said I hadn't seen any dragon girls. That I didn't even know what a dragon girl *was*."

Emba let out a long sigh of relief. *Thank goodness. You had me worried there for a moment.*

But Odolf wasn't finished yet. "And then I er... er..."

"You '*er*' *what?*" demanded Emba. She didn't like the shifty look in her friend's eye or his renewed interest in the rug. There was something he wasn't telling them. Something bad.

"I might have mentioned something about a girl with scales," he mumbled. "And there's a chance I might have told him where to find her…"

"A chance?" said Fred. "How much of a chance?"

"Quite a strong chance," he admitted. "I'm really sorry. How was I to know though? I'd never even heard of this Necromalcolm fellow until now. I was just trying to be helpful."

"Helpful?" repeated Emba. "*Helpful?* Perhaps you could have invited him back here for some acorn ale while you were at it? Maybe you could have helped bundle me into the sack." Was that what evil sorcerers and their bearded henchmen did to girls with dragon blood? Bundle them up and carry them off to their wicked lairs? Or did they slice them open on the spot and drain the blood out there and then? "And you didn't think to say anything until now?" she went on, growing more incredulous—and more terrified—with every passing word. "Not even when I told you there was someone watching me? It was probably *him*. Watching and waiting, ready to attack." She shivered again. Perhaps it would have been better if the dragon *had* carried her off, like the one in her dreams.

"Hush now, Emba dear," said Fred. "What's done is done. Odolf didn't mean you any harm, did you?"

Odolf shook his head. He looked like he was about to cry. "Of course I didn't. You're like a sister to me."

"What's important now is that we all stick together," said Fred firmly. "And make sure we keep Emba safe. When *was* this, Odolf? When did you meet this bearded man of yours?"

Odolf thought for a moment. A rather long moment that involved squeezing his eyes shut, biting his bottom lip, and counting on his fingers. "Five or six days ago?" he said, at last, as if it was a question rather than a statement of fact. As if it was a fireside game of 'What am I?' they were playing, rather than a life-and-death round of 'Who's Coming for Emba's Blood?'.

"Five or six days," Fred murmured. "That's good. If he hasn't stolen you away yet that means the charm's working. It means we've got time to work out a proper plan to keep you safe."

Or it means he's still busy polishing his special dragon-blood-collecting cup, thought Emba. *Busy sharpening his knife...* She clutched at the leather pouch around her neck, wishing she shared Fred's optimism. Could the old lady's toenails *really* be that powerful? Powerful enough to keep away an evil sorcerer? But wait, Fred said the pouch was to keep her hidden from the scrying bowl. That meant there must be another charm too, another toenail off-cut secreted somewhere around the cave. It could be hidden inside her hair-stuffed mattress—that might explain why it was so scratchy and uncomfortable. Or nestling with the goose feathers inside her pillow? Or... or... or maybe Fred had been grinding up bits of toenail and slipping them into her food... Emba almost gagged at the thought.

"But it won't be enough to keep him away forever," said Fred. "I think it's time we consulted the Tome and found out exactly what we're dealing with." She hauled herself onto her feet with a loud creaking in her knees, and hobbled over to the concealed stone recess at the back of the cave. She tugged aside the crudely made wall hanging—Emba could never decide if the woven picture was a misshapen bird or a misshapen lion—and pulled out the ancient book hidden behind it, wheezing with the effort. The Tome of Terrible Tomorrows was as big and heavy as it was old. It was always dusty too somehow, no matter how long it had been since Fred had last consulted it. Which was why every consultation began the same way—with blowing away the layer of white dust off the front cover to reveal the awful eight-legged sea monster design waiting underneath.

Fred brought the book over to her consulting table and blew away the dust, as normal. But her face was drawn and her fingers were shaking, which definitely *wasn't* normal. As for her left eye—that was twitching so hard it was a wonder she could see anything out of it at all.

"*I call on you, oh Ancient Tome,*" Fred intoned, as she always did,

"*To show me what will be,*
Those Terrible Tomorrows
That await inside of thee.

Reveal to me the dreaded course
The cruel Fates have decreed
For she who stands before you now,
Your supplicant in need."

Emba must have listened to those exact same words hundreds of times before—she could probably recite them in her sleep—but now that *she* was the supplicant in need, it felt like she was hearing them for the first time. Why did it have to be *a dreaded course* lying in store for her? What was wrong with a *cheerful* course or a *wonderful* one? Why were the Fates always cruel, come to that?

She watched as the old woman's face changed, her eyes rolling up inside their sockets until only the whites were visible. Even after all this time, the sight of her beloved guardian's features twisting and changing under the Tome's spell still gave Emba the creeps. She couldn't tear her eyes away though. This was *her* future coursing through Fred's stiffened body. It was *her* fate sending the old woman's head rocking back and forth on her wrinkled neck.

Fred's mouth slipped open, revealing a handful

of yellow teeth and shrivelled gums, her grey-tinged tongue lolling fat and useless, like a limp slumpfish. Her breath became laboured as the Powers of Dreadful Divination took their toll, a thin line of drool dribbling out the side of her mouth and trickling down her chin whiskers. But Fred didn't seem to notice. Her fingers were too busy flicking through the gold-edged pages of the Tome, waiting for the right prophecy to reveal itself.

And there it was. Fred let out a sudden shuddering gasp, her hands flying backwards from the book as if they'd been burned. Her eyes rolled back into position, the muscles of her face returning to normal. Her lips moved soundlessly as she peered at the open page before her, reading and rereading the spidery text.

"Well now," she said at last. "That's interesting."

Good interesting or bad interesting, wondered Emba. "What is?" she asked. "What does it say?"

"Hm?" Fred looked up in surprise, as if she'd forgotten the others were there. "Ah yes, well that's the thing. The issue isn't what it says. It's what it *doesn't* say."

Chapter 5

The Terrible Tomorrow

Fred cleared her throat.

"*She who would stay safe from harm,*" she read,

"*May find her safety fled,*

Though stone walls hold her tight in sleep,

Secure and sound in bed.

She who fights with truth and nail

By truth and love is lost,

As she who would stay safe from harm

May find out to her cost."

"So as long as Emba's got stone walls to hold her safe in sleep, she'll be secure and sound?" said Odolf. "Phew! That's alright then."

"Weren't you listening?" snapped Emba, irritated by his blind optimism in the face of danger. *Her* danger, that was. Not his. Odolf might not be so chirpy if it was *his* life on the line. If *he* was the one waiting to be kidnapped by a dragon-blood-thirsty necromancer. "What about 'may find her safety fled'?" she said. "What about 'by truth and love is lost'? They don't sound very alright to me."

"Hm," said Fred again. "I think Odolf has a point. You'll be safe enough as long as you stay within the stone walls of the cave—that's the important part. That's what we need to focus on tonight. As for the rest… well, time will tell, I suppose. Who are we to guess at the Tome's meaning?"

What do you mean, 'who are we to guess'? thought Emba, staring at Fred in disbelief. *You're the Wise Hermit of Witchingford Wood, the Tome's appointed guardian! The official unraveller of its riddles!* "But you don't need to guess at its meaning," she said out loud. "You know what it is. You always do. That's what makes you so wise."

"And her toenails, of course," cut in Odolf. "The source of untold wisdom and power. Don't forget about them."

Emba ignored him. "Besides," she told Fred, "it's not what the prophecy said that's the issue. It's what it *didn't* say. That's what you told us a minute ago."

"Did I?" said Fred, with an unconvincing look of surprise. "Well now, that was... er... that was before I had time to consider it properly. But now that I have, I can't see any cause for concern. You'll notice it only says 'may': '*May* find her safety fled. *May* find out to her cost. Which means there's a chance we'll avoid all that. It means that as long as our defences are in place you'll be perfectly safe here. Really, Emba dear, there's nothing for you to worry about."

But Emba *was* worried. If everything was as alright as all that, why was Fred's eye still twitching? Why did she keep clutching at her heart? And why was Emba's own heart pounding inside her chest?

It was still pounding when they turned in for the night. When Odolf took his leave, heading back to his treetop shelter with his usual cheery whistle, as if it was just another night at the end of another day. As if the world hadn't shifted on its axis, turning everything upside-down. What did it all mean? The egg... the dragon… Did Emba *really* have dragon blood flowing through her veins? That explained the strange scales on her arms and legs. But where was her tail? Where were her wings? And what about her real parents? Were they dragons too? Had they been looking for her all this time? Or had they abandoned the egg in disgust, knowing there was something wrong with the baby growing inside? And what about Necromalcolm? How did he fit into all of this? How did he even know she existed?

Emba's heart was still pounding as she drank her evening goat's milk. As she settled down on her hair-stuffed mattress and pulled the rough blankets up round her chin. As Fred sang the same nightly lullaby she'd been singing since Emba was small, her voice as warbling and tuneless as always. That's if you could call such a dark, disturbing rhyme a lullaby…

"Keep me safe in sleep tonight
From murderous tooth and claw,
From flashing blade and bloodied sword
And monsters bathed in gore.
Keep me safe from crunching jaws,

From eyes like burning coals,
Protect me as I dream tonight
From evil hearts and souls.
Keep me safe by moon, by sun,
Whenever danger calls,
Bind me from all harm and hold me
Safe within these walls."

The familiar words sounded different tonight though. They sounded more menacing than usual. More loaded with meaning. Emba lay there, listening in the flickering candlelight, her heart still pounding.

"It's not a lullaby at all, is it?" she asked, once Fred had finished. "It's the other charm you were talking about before." It all made sense now.

Fred nodded. "A bit of both, maybe," she said. "It always helped you slip off to sleep when you were little. And it helped *me* sleep better, knowing that you were safe."

Emba couldn't imagine slipping off to sleep at all tonight. Not with so many wild thoughts and fears whirring round inside her head. Not with Necromalcolm out there, searching for her. Coming for her. "But what if it's not strong enough? What if magic words and toenails aren't enough to stop him?"

"You'll be perfectly safe as long as you stay here in the cave," said Fred, drawing her into a warm hug and kissing the top of her head. "Trust me. The best thing you can do now is shut your eyes and get a good night's sleep. Everything will seem better in the morning, you'll see."

"But..."

"No," said Fred, firmly. "No more buts. No more ifs. You need your rest now. We both do. You snuggle down and shut your eyes, and I'll sing it one more time to help you drop off. How does that sound?"

As far as Emba was concerned it sounded downright impossible. How was she supposed to drop off after so many life-changing revelations? But she did as she was told, not wanting to add to her guardian's own list of worries. Maybe Fred was right. Maybe everything *would* seem better in the morning. Emba closed her eyes, letting the sinister words of the lullaby-charm wash over her one more time.

Keep me safe in sleep tonight, from murderous tooth

and claw... Dark dragons flitted and flamed behind her eyelids as Fred's quavering voice drifted through the inky blackness. And then came the soft, muted clash of bloodied swords. Such dark, heavy swords... Whose blood was that, anyway, Emba wondered... Her blood? Dragon blood? So much blood... And then the monsters... only the monsters never quite came... and then... And then the words faded away to a deep velvety nothing as the lullaby worked its usual magic...

Emba's dragon came back for her that night. Her dream dragon, that was, swooping into her sleeping mind with its gleaming talons and its bone-threaded wings beating against the black sky. It scooped her up in its long, polished claws—just like it had every other night—and carried her off into the darkness. The wild rushing sensation in her stomach as they took flight felt exactly the same too—a curious mixture of fear and exhilaration—but that was where the similarities ended. Because it wasn't just the one dragon tonight, she realised with a sickening lurch. There was another one chasing after them—a whirling swirl of dragon-shaped smoke—with red gleaming eyes. The exact same red colour as the cracked hole in the sky opening up in front of them, as if it was waiting to swallow them whole. That was new too. Even in her dream, Emba knew that wasn't right. That none of it was right. But it was too late to try and make sense of it because the smoke dragon was already upon them, its dark, choking cloud of a body swirling round her as they flew... Except somehow Emba *wasn't* flying anymore. She was falling... falling, plummeting through the air like a stone, the ground screaming up to meet her. Or maybe Emba was the one screaming...

SMACK!

Emba crashed back into wakefulness, her entire body bathed in sweat, her ragged breath catching in the throbbing soreness of her throat.

It was just a dream, she told herself, as the panic eased away again. As her eyes adjusted to the dawn gloom and she found herself safe and sound in her own bed. The events of the previous evening felt like a dream too now—like a fireside tale of imaginary beasts and doomed heroes. But there *was* no doom. Necromalcolm hadn't come for her in the night after all. Her blood was still in her veins where it belonged, pumping round her body like normal. Nothing had changed. She touched her fingers to her leather pouch and smiled. But Emba couldn't have been more wrong. *Everything* had changed. She just didn't know it yet.

Chapter 6

The Dreadful Discovery of Doom

The quietness was the clue. Or it should have been, if Emba was thinking clearly. Every morning, without fail, she awoke to the sound of snoring—to a one-woman symphony of animal snorts and nasal whistles. Sharing her sleeping quarters with Fred was like sharing a room with a wild boar. A boar with a blocked nose and a rattle stuck in its throat. Yes, every morning Emba would lie there in the gloom, listening to the impressive rumbles and growls, marvelling afresh at how much noise could come out of one old lady's mouth. Every morning until now.

It wasn't until she got up to use the old tin bucket that served as a chamber pot that Emba realised what was missing. *Who* was missing.

"Fred?" she called, forgetting all about her bladder in the sudden rush of fear that took hold of her. But there was no answer. Even in the murky gloom of the inner cave, Emba could tell that her guardian's bed was empty.

Perhaps she left early this morning, to collect some more herbs, Emba tried telling herself. But the twisting clench in her guts and the hot, burning sensation in her chest told her otherwise. *Something's happened. Something bad.*

Emba swapped her nightshirt for her tunic and wriggled through the crawl hole, hoping against hope that she was wrong. But there was no sign of Fred out in the main cave either. No sign of life at all. The ashes of the previous night's fire lay cold and dead— abandoned and forgotten in the wake of everything that had happened.

Wait, what was that dark red patch on the floor by Fred's stool? It looked like… yes, it looked like blood! Was it Fred's? Was she hurt? The twisting clench in Emba's guts was stronger than ever as she hurried over for a closer look, calling as she went.

"Fred? Fred? Where are you?"

It was only a small patch but still large enough to confirm Emba's worst fears. Fred was in trouble. Perhaps she'd been attacked by wild animals and carried off into the woods. Or thieves, hoping to harness the prophetic wisdom of the Tome for their own ends, or... or maybe Necromalcolm's henchman had come looking for Emba in the dark and taken Fred by mistake. He must have knocked her out with something sharp—that would explain the blood—and then bundled her up into a sack while she was out cold.

"Fred!" Emba called again, racing to the cave entrance as if she might still catch her. "FRED! Where are you?"

There was no answer.

"FREDDDDDDDDDD!" Hot tears streamed down Emba's cheeks as she stood screaming into the morning air. "FREDDDDDDDDD!"

"I'm coming," called Odolf, charging out of the woods towards her, with his helmet in one hand and a long sharpened stick in the other, like a spear.

"Odolf Bravebuckle to the rescue! What is it? What's happened?"

Emba wiped her eyes and took a deep breath, but it was a while before she could get any proper words out. "It's F-F-Fred," she finally managed. "She's g-g-gone. And there's b-blood on the floor and... and... look!" she gasped, spotting long marks in the mud, stretching away from the cave entrance. There were two of them—deep, scuffled lines made by feet dragging against the earth—and a trail of heavy-booted footprints running alongside.

"I knew it," said Emba, her eyes welling up again at the thought of her guardian being dragged through the mud like a sack of firewood. "Somebody m-must have taken her. And not just *one* somebody, either. Look! Two different sets of footprints. Big footprints at that. Poor Fred. She wouldn't have stood a chance." If only Fred had put a protective charm on *herself* too. But then magic didn't work like that—that's what she'd always told Emba. At least *good* magic didn't. Good magic required love and sacrifice as well as skill and learning. It couldn't be used for selfish ends. And now

Fred had made the ultimate sacrifice, by getting carted off in Emba's place.

"Necromalcolm's henchmen," said Odolf, looking less heroic and brave by the second. The colour had drained from his face and his sharpened stick was shaking in his hand. "They must have come to the cave looking for you, after I opened my big mouth, and taken her instead. It's all my fault."

Yes, thought Emba. *It is.* But there was no time for blame now. It was time for action. "At least we know which way they went," she said, pulling herself together and drying her eyes again. "Come on," she added. "The sooner we find where they've taken Fred, the sooner we can save her."

She sprinted off into the woods without waiting for a response, following the trail of footprints in the direction of the river. Odolf was right behind her though. Emba could hear the slap of his feet against the wet ground, and the huff and pant of his breath as he raced to catch her up.

Cold mud squelched between her toes as she ran. Sharp sticks and fallen nuts scratched at the soles of her feet, stinging nettle clumps brushing against her hands as she careered past, but Emba barely noticed. She was too focused on following the footprints and finding Fred. So focused, in fact, that she didn't spot the snare tree up ahead, or the roots that came snaking out of the ground as she approached—not until it was too late. Not until the gnarled tendrils had already fastened themselves round her foot, stopping her in her tracks. There was never a *good* time to get trapped by snare roots—of course there wasn't. Not unless you *liked* having your blood sucked by a carnivorous tree. But this, it had to be said, was a spectacularly *bad* time for it to happen.

"Aagghhhh! Get off!" she screamed.

"What is it?" Odolf came to a panting halt beside her. "Are you alright?"

"Snare root," Emba cried, wincing with pain as the root's tiny hairs threaded their way into her skin like needle-sharp tongues. "Ow, ow, ow! Get it off me, please."

Odolf leapt into action, pulling back his homemade spear with a loud grunt of effort and thrusting it into the thick, heaving body of the root, a mere inch or so from Emba's foot. "Take that!" he cried.

Emba flinched as the spear struck its target. There was a horrid hissing squeal and a smell of burning vegetation, and then the root finally let go of her foot, slithering back into the ground to await its next victim.

"Thank you," she gasped, limping safely out of the tree's reach.

Odolf grinned, lifting off his helmet and dropping down into a low bow. "Odolf Bravebuckle at your service." But when he straightened back up again, his grin had vanished. "Will you still be able to walk on it?" he asked anxiously.

"It's fine. I'm alright," Emba lied, staring down at her swollen foot which had turned a fetching shade of purple. "At least I will be in a minute." But it took all of her self-control not to cry out loud in pain when she tried putting any weight on it. "I can't believe I was so stupid," she said. "Running right up to a snare tree like that. I was so busy following the trail, I didn't see it." The line of footprints alongside the snare's pulsing trunk suggested she wasn't the only one to make that mistake. But either it was still dark when Fred's kidnappers came past, which meant the snare tree would have been sleeping, or they'd managed to fight it off too. *With their weapons*, Emba thought miserably, imagining long sharp blades capable of bleeding a poor old lady dry. *Or some horrible dark magic*. She wasn't sure which one was worse.

"Here." Odolf offered her his homemade spear-slash-snare root stabber as a walking stick. "Try this."

"Thank you." *Ow!* "Yes, that's better," Emba pretended. Every step was agony but she limped on determinedly, refusing to give up. Emba Oak wasn't a giving-up kind of girl, especially not when someone she loved was in danger. Besides, she'd listened to enough epic adventures round the fire to know that rescue quests were never easy. There were obstacles at every turn. But then most rescue quests didn't grind to a halt quite as soon as theirs seemed destined to...

"Oh no," said Odolf, pointing ahead. "Look at the prints. They must have had horses tied up here, waiting for them, where no one would see."

Emba hobbled to catch him up, hoping he was

wrong. But yes, those were horse prints alright. *Curses. Fred could be miles away by now.*

The hoofprints continued down to the river path, where they joined countless other hoofprints stretching away in both directions. Emba stared at the crisscrossed trails, trying (and failing) to tell them apart, before slumping down onto a nearby rock in defeat. Fred always told her to look on the bright side when things got tough. But there *was* no bright side. Fred was gone—whisked away on horseback—and they couldn't even tell which direction the kidnappers had taken, let alone catch them.

Chapter 7

The Nefarious Note of Nastiness

What would Fred do if one of us had gone missing? Emba asked herself as she made her painful way back home, trying to work out their next move. *How would she go about finding us?* And then it struck her. *The Tome of Terrible Tomorrows! Of course!* The Tome knew *everything*. Whether it would be willing to share its knowledge with Emba was a different matter, but it had to be worth a try. She hobbled into the cave after Odolf, feeling slightly more hopeful than she had a few moments before. "I've got an idea," she said.

"And I've got a note," he replied, holding up a soggy-looking scroll of paper. "The kidnappers must have left it for you. It's from Necromalcolm."

"What? Where did you find that? What does it say?"

Emba didn't wait for an answer, snatching it out of his hand to see for herself.

Dear Dragon Girl, it said, in spidery, ink-splotted handwriting.

I trust that my faithful servants have fulfilled their task and your guardian has been suitably kidnapped, as per my cunning plan.

If you want to save the old crone from a dreadful fate – a fate so dreadful and calamitous that I don't even know how to spell it – you'd better come t̶̶̶̶̶̶̶̶̶̶̶̶̶̶̶̶ to save her, before it's too late.

Yours impatiently,
Necromalcolm

"Come to where?" said Emba, staring at the big black ink smudge. She tried rubbing it with her finger but that only made things worse. Now it was an even bigger smudge.

"It was like that when I found it, I swear," said Odolf,

before she could accuse him of anything. He pointed to a random spot on the floor. "It was down there, with a stone on top to keep it from blowing away." Emba must have been too busy staring at the blood by the fire to notice it before. Too busy rushing out of the cave in tears. "Right under that dripping stalactite," he added. "You'd think Necromalcolm might have spotted that in his porridge bowl and warned them, wouldn't you? No wait, it wasn't porridge, was it? It was..."

"Shhh," hissed Emba. "I'm trying to think." There was no shortage of thoughts swirling round her head—*What did Necromalcolm mean, 'before it's too late'? How long have we got left? What sort of fate is even harder to spell than 'calamitous'? And what does 'calamitous' even mean?*—but they weren't particularly useful ones. They weren't the fool-proof-plan sort of thoughts she was after.

"Oh yes," said Odolf. "Your big idea. What was it?"

"Huh?" *Now* what was he talking about?

"Just before," said Odolf. "You said you had an

idea, and then I said I had a note."

"Of course, that's it!" said Emba. "We can ask the Tome of Terrible Tomorrows where they're keeping Fred."

Even though Emba had grown up with the Tome— it was as much a part of her life with Fred as the old lady's potions and charms and warm comforting hugs—she'd never attempted to read it before. She'd never even touched it. Her hands were trembling as she tugged aside the wall-hanging and reached for the ancient volume.

Oof! No wonder Fred struggled sometimes—it weighed a tonne! Emba staggered over to the Tome-consulting table and dropped the book down with a grunt of relief. A fresh layer of white dust had settled on the cover again, hiding the eight-legged sea monster lurking underneath. Emba blew it away, just like Fred always did.

"Are you sure about this?" asked Odolf, looking doubtful. "How will you know what the prophecy means once you find it?"

"I'll know," said Emba firmly, sounding more

confident than she felt. At least she knew the summoning words—that was a good start:

"*I call on you, oh ancient tome*
To show me what will be,
Those Terrible Tomorrows
That wait inside of thee."

They sounded strange coming out of her own mouth though. Strange and wrong. Would the Tome realise she wasn't Fred? Would the summoning still work? But Emba brushed her doubts aside and carried on.

"*Reveal to me the dreaded course*
The cruel Fates have decreed
For she who stands before you now,
Your supplicant in need."

There. Now what? Emba waited for the horrible facial contortions to start. For her eyes to roll up inside their sockets like Fred's always did. But her face—and eyes—felt like normal. Her head didn't start rocking backwards and forwards, and her mouth stayed firmly shut. There was no sign of any dribble running down into Emba's chin whiskers either. Not that she *had* any chin whiskers.

"Nothing's happening," whispered Odolf. "Maybe it's not just about *saying* the right words. Maybe you have to *think* them too."

"What do you mean?"

Odolf shrugged. "I don't know exactly. But were you thinking about Fred when you did the summoning? I mean *really* thinking about her."

Emba closed the book, screwing up her face with concentration as she pictured her adoptive mother. She pictured the soft, kind grey of her eyes and the silver tangle of her hair; the deep smile lines etched into the old woman's cheeks and the crinkly wrinkles in her forehead. She pictured her yellow teeth and her equally yellow toenails, tap-tap-tapping on the cave floor, and the comforting scent of herbs clinging to her age-worn skin. She thought about the warmth of her arms holding Emba tight whenever she was scared, or sad, or hurt.

There was a lump in her throat as she imagined how scared Fred must be right now, with no one to hold *her* tight and tell her everything was going to be alright. Tears seeped from her closed eyes as she imagined

Fred hurt and bleeding.

"I call on you, oh ancient tome," she tried again, the words little more than a hoarse whisper this time. "To show me what will be…" She pictured Fred with her hands pinned behind her back, as Necromalcolm's henchmen pushed and jostled her like an animal. *Please show me where they've taken her*, she begged, silently, as she reached the last line. *Tell me what I have to do to save her.*

Woah! There was a blinding burst of light behind her eyes, like a lightning flash, and a tight twisting sensation in her head. It felt like icy hands reaching in through her ears—right into her skull—and forcing everything out of place. Like cold iron fists grabbing hold of everything she'd ever known and squeezing it tight. Tighter and tighter they squeezed, as she shook her head backwards and forwards to escape their grip. But there *was* no escape.

Emba was dimly aware of something cold and wet trickling out of her open mouth as she fought to breathe. But she had no control over her body anymore. Her fingers felt like they belonged to someone else as they leafed through the pages of the Tome again, flicking them over faster and faster and—

HERRGH!

Emba gasped out loud as a fierce rush of air was sucked back into her lungs, her hands shooting away from the book as if it was on fire. She stared down at the Tome in shock. Did that mean it had worked? Was the prophecy in front of her the one that would lead her to Fred?

"Phew," said Odolf. "That was wild! Are you alright? Did it hurt? Can I have a go? Maybe it will show me the Final Prophecy and prove that *I'm* the hero the world is waiting for."

But Emba didn't answer. She was too busy reading the Tome. Too busy turning the words over and over in her head, trying to make sense of them. "Ire," she murmured. "What does that mean?"

"Ire? Here, let me see," said Odolf, peering over her shoulder.

"*Safety lies in walls of stone,*" he read.

"*In promises to keep,*

A stolen heart and broken art

Lies weeping in the deep.
Freedom calls the one who seeks
In tongues of pain and fire,
Bonds shall break and shackles shake
Before the hero's ire.

"Perhaps it's short for iron?" he suggested. "Something to do with armour... or... or maybe it's an iron belt buckle! What if *I'm* the hero who'll break Fred's bonds?" He pulled himself up tall and straightened his helmet.

"I suppose it *could* mean that," agreed Emba. "Though that still doesn't help with finding her in the first place."

But Odolf was on a roll now. "And the bit about tongues of pain and fire," he added. "That sounds like the Final Prophecy: *A hero forged in fiercest flame, a child of iron and pain.* I *knew* it was about me. I just knew it." He was growing more excited by the second. "This could be the moment I've been waiting for. The chance to finally prove myself... To heal the chasm and save the kingdom from being torn in two..."

"But what about Fred?" asked Emba, trying to steer

him back to the task in hand. *Safety lies in walls of stone...* Could 'safety' be a Tome-riddle word for Fred herself? She'd certainly done a good job of protecting Emba all these years. "Walls of stone could be anywhere," she sighed. "What about the weeping in the deep part? What do you think that means?"

"It could be a dungeon, I suppose... with walls of stone... and shackles... That's what they call the prisoners' chains," Odolf said, with surprising authority on the subject.

Emba didn't want to think about Fred lying in some dark, rat-infested dungeon, with her legs in chains. But that was all she *could* think about now. *I'll get you out of there if it's the last thing I do*, she promised. She might not be a hero-in-waiting like Odolf, with a special helmet and belt buckle, but that didn't mean she couldn't fight. It didn't mean she wouldn't risk everything to save Fred from Necromalcolm's evil clutches. *As soon as we work out where this dungeon is...*

Odolf tapped his finger against the page. "And look at this line here," he said. "'In promises to keep'.

I don't know what the promise bit means, but 'keep' is what they call the fortified tower in a castle…"

"So she's in a dungeon underneath the castle tower," said Emba. "That's it! What are we waiting for then?"

Odolf looked a whole lot less keen on saving the day in a blaze of glory, all of a sudden. "*The* castle?" he said. "As in Gravethorn Castle?"

Emba nodded. "I don't know of any other ones. Do you?"

"No," admitted Odolf. "But why would Necromalcolm have her taken *there?*"

"I don't know," said Emba. "Maybe his evil lair doesn't have a dungeon. Or… or maybe he's been staying at the castle while he's looking for me. Perhaps it's just nearer…" *And it has to be somewhere near so that I'll be able to reach her*, she realised with a shiver. It was a trap, wasn't it? Necromalcolm didn't need to kidnap Emba. He didn't need to break the protective charm Fred wove around her every night. He could simply take Fred, instead, leaving Emba to come chasing after her… right into his necromancing clutches.

You'll be safe as long as you stay in the cave. That's what Fred had said. But they'd never save her that way. No. Emba clenched her fists. Staying put was no longer an option.

"If the Tome says she's in the castle, then that's where she'll be," she said firmly. "It's never been wrong yet."

"But…" Odolf protested. "But…"

"But what? What happened to 'Odolf Bravebuckle to the rescue'? I thought this was your big chance to prove what a hero you are." Emba studied him, carefully. "You're not *scared*, are you?" she asked, trying not to let the fear show on her own face. Who *wouldn't* be scared at the prospect of breaking into a heavily guarded castle to rescue a prisoner from the dungeons?

Odolf sighed. "Of course not," he said, looking positively terrified. "The thing is… I er…" He sighed again, fingering the iron dragon on his belt buckle. "It's a long story…"

Chapter 8

The Terribly Long Tale of Odolf Bravebuckle

There was no time for one of Odolf's endless stories.

"You've got as long as it takes for me to sort out my swollen foot," said Emba. "I need to find some of Fred's swellbalm and comfrey lotion, otherwise I'll be limping all the way." It was going to be difficult enough rescuing her guardian on *two* legs, let alone one.

Odolf sat down on Fred's stool by the fire—despite the fact that the fire was nothing more than a pile of white ashes—and cleared his throat.

"Well," he began at last, "like all the best stories and adventures, this one starts with a knock at the door. With a mysterious, shadowy stranger, bringing danger and peril in their wake. First the knocking—the sharp rap of bony knuckles against waiting wood—and then the life-changing quest…"

"Yes, yes, I know what a knock at the door sounds like," said Emba, trying to speed him up. The thought of Fred all alone in the dark dungeon was almost too much to bear. "*Everyone* knows that. Forget about the knocking and get to the castle part."

"This *is* the castle part," Odolf replied, indignantly. "It was a castle door he was knocking on. Well, a door in the castle grounds… It was one of the duchess's soldiers, knocking on the forge door. He said that his mistress wanted to see my master, to discuss designs for a special…"

"Ah, here we are! Found it!" Emba held up the pot of lotion in triumph. "Seriously, hurry up Odolf," she begged as she got to work, dipping her fingers into the cool green gloop and smearing it over her foot. The sooner they were on the road, the sooner they'd reach Fred. "Just give me the quick version for now."

Chapter 8 [Revisited]

The Terribly Truncated Tale of Odolf Bravebuckle

"Fine," said Odolf, with a sigh. "You know when I first arrived in Witchingford Wood, and I told you I'd run away from my master, the blacksmith, because he was cruel and heartless?"

"Yes," replied Emba, rubbing in the lotion. *Ah, that feels better already.* "I remember. What about him?"

"I lied," said Odolf. "Not about him being cruel and heartless—he was certainly both of those things—but that wasn't why I ran away. I stole something that didn't belong to me. *That's* the real reason I had to leave."

"I know. You stole the helmet," said Emba, dismissively. "It's not exactly a secret."

"But I took something else too," said Odolf. "My

dragon belt buckle. I didn't mean to—I was only trying it on, but then I heard them coming and I ran. It wasn't just any old buckle, you see. The duchess had designed it herself as a birthday present for her brother. My master said we had to make sure it was the best belt buckle anyone had ever forged if we wanted to keep our heads on our shoulders."

Odolf traced the dragon outline with his fingertip. "All those little details—the curling tail and the scaled wings—it all had to be perfect. Like I said, my master was a cruel man, but he was a pussy cat compared to the duchess. They say she killed her own husband just to get her hands on his dukedom." Odolf shivered. "I don't think my master was joking about us losing our heads if we got anything wrong. He wasn't really a joking sort of man."

"What were you doing with her belt buckle then, if she was as dangerous as all that?"

Odolf shook his head. "I don't know," he said. "I don't know what came over me. But it was so beautiful and shiny. So powerful. I think it must have been something to do with the special powder I saw my master adding to the fire—something the duchess had given him in secret. It made the flames turn green and snakelike, and it did something strange to the metal too. It was like it was singing." He wrinkled up his nose. "No, singing's not the right word. It was like it was calling to me. Like it *wanted* me to thread it onto my own belt and see how it felt. Not to keep though—that was never the plan. I was going to put it straight back afterwards. Only my master returned sooner than I thought... and he wasn't alone."

"The duchess?" guessed Emba.

Odolf nodded. "And there *I* was, prancing round the workshop wearing her brother's buckle and a helmet we'd taken in for repairs. I was pretending to be a knight," he said, blushing at the memory. "But then I heard voices coming along the path and I panicked. If it was just my master on his own that would have been bad enough—he'd have beaten me until I couldn't sit down for a week—but I could hear another voice too. A lady's voice. 'Let's hope you've done justice to my design, she was saying. My brother is very particular when it comes to dragons. '

"I didn't hang around to hear any more. I was already halfway out the back door. I didn't even look back to see if they'd spotted me. I just ran. I've never run so fast in my life. Or so far. Even when it got too dark to see, I kept on running."

"But they must have sent soldiers after you as soon as the theft was discovered," said Emba. "How did you manage to outrun them if they were on horseback? How come they didn't catch you?"

Odolf shrugged. "It must have been the belt protecting me. There's something magic about it, I know there is. Or maybe it was fate. Maybe I was *always* destined to be a hero, just like in the prophecy. Maybe it was fate that led me here, to Witchingford Wood. To you and Fred, and the Tome of Terrible Tomorrows."

"And does it still work?" asked Emba. "The belt's magic, I mean. Is it still protecting you? Because it didn't do a very good job of it that time the boar gouged you in the stomach."

"That's because I wasn't wearing it," said Odolf. "I'd taken it off to go for a swim. The belt's magic is as strong as ever—I'm sure of it. It's the secret of my fearsome courage, you know. It's what puts the 'brave' in Odolf Bravebuckle."

"Well in that case, Odolf Bravebuckle should be perfectly safe going *back* to the castle too," said Emba. "Come on, you and me together, what do you say? A dragon girl and a boy with a magic buckle—it sounds like the perfect hermit-rescuing team to me. But we need to leave *now*. No more stories," she added. "No more false starts. It's time for action."

Chapter 9

The Remorseless River of Ruin

The swellbalm and comfrey lotion had done wonders for Emba's foot, which was back to its normal size and colour already. It barely hurt at all now, which was just as well given how much walking they still had ahead of them.

Maybe we'll be lucky and find a passing cart once we get out of the woods, Emba thought as she trudged along the riverbank, keeping a sharp eye out for snare roots and boulder-beasts. She was *pretty* sure boulder-beasts only existed in stories—the sort of stories where children got carried off by hulking great creatures with rock-like bodies and three rows of sharp teeth—but that's exactly what she'd thought about dragons until one landed outside her non-existent door.

They'd been following the river for hours now. Long, thankless hours of picking their way through the undergrowth, clambering over fallen logs and mysterious moss-covered rocks (none of which turned out to have any teeth). Emba's foot might have been feeling better, but her legs were starting to ache.

"How much further do you think, until we strike off towards the road?" she asked.

"About three hundred yards less than the last time you asked," said Odolf, casting an anxious glance over his shoulder. His hero swagger had all but vanished at the prospect of returning to the castle. He'd been in a strange, nervous mood all day, jumping at every hooting bird and breaking twig, squealing out loud at a ghostly glowing face through the trees. Except it wasn't a face at all—it was a swarm of beaming wish bugs, bathing their wings in the cool forest air. They scattered at the sound of Odolf's cry, vanishing back into the shadows before Emba had a chance to catch one, taking their unclaimed wishes with them. *Curses.* But she wished all the same, pressing her hands into tightly-balled fists as if she could squeeze some of the bugs' soft glowing magic out of her own clenched fingers, whispering under her breath. "Please let Fred be alright. Please let us get to her in time."

Emba was feeling increasingly nervous too—Odolf's twitchiness must have been catching. What if Necromalcolm never meant for them to reach the castle, once he'd got them safely out of the cave? What if his men were following after them at that very moment…?

She clutched at her leather pouch as something rustled in the undergrowth. What was that? A henchman? A soldier? A boulder-beast? No, a squirrel. Emba laughed out loud as it tore past her, dashing from branch to branch like a red streak of flame.

"Shhh," hissed Odolf. "I can hear something."

A second squirrel followed hot on its companion's heels, and a flock of screech finches took to the sky, screaming up from the treetops. Something must have spooked them. The eerie silence that followed was enough to spook Emba too.

She shrank back against the nearest tree as a loud cry broke the quiet: "Look, there! Up ahead!" That was no squirrel.

"Soldiers!" whispered Odolf. "Get down!"

Emba dropped into a low crouch, ignoring the sting of nettles as she pressed herself in tight against the trunk. What were soldiers doing so far from the castle? Had they come for Odolf? *He* clearly thought so. He was trembling all over, his hands clasped tight over his dragon belt buckle. Emba wanted to reach out and touch his shaking shoulders and tell him everything was going to be alright. But she wasn't altogether sure it *was* going to be alright. Her own shoulders were shaking too, her heart thumping against her ribcage as she strained her ears for approaching danger.

She could hear the sound of the soldiers' oars moving through the water towards them now, accompanied by low grunts of exertion. Somehow she'd assumed they'd be on foot, or on horseback— like soldiers in stories—but arriving by boat didn't make them any less terrifying. Emba reached inside her goatskin bag for her scaring-off stone, her shaking fingers fumbling to find it. It wouldn't be much help against fully-grown soldiers with sharp swords, but that was all she had: a stone, a sheep's bladder flask of water and some honey and quince scones. Oh yes, and a blanket. If only she could *picnic* her way out of danger…

"There! You grab the skinny one," came a second, higher-pitched cry, "and I'll take that big ugly one there!"

Somehow, even through her fear, Emba still managed to feel confused and offended. She and Odolf were *both* pretty small and skinny. As for describing one of them as 'ugly'… well, that was just plain rude. Maybe Odolf was offended too. Maybe that was what tipped him over the edge, turning him from a trembling, cowering mess into a reckless blaze of energy, leaping out from his hiding place with a ferocious warlike cry.

"You'll never take us alive!" he roared.

What? Emba wasn't sure she liked the sound of that. Being taken alive sounded much better than being taken dead. But Odolf wasn't finished yet. "Odolf Bravebuckle never surrenders!" he cried. And then came a pause. "Wait a minute, you're not soldiers."

They weren't? Emba peered out from behind her tree to see a family of river catchers crowded into a broad-bottomed boat beside a cage of still-wriggling eels and giant water spiders. *Phew! Thank goodness for that!*

"Soldiers?" laughed one of the raggedy children. "No, we passed them ages ago," she said, pointing along the river, "cutting down trees for the duchess's new execution block. They say she's worn the old one out with all that head-chopping."

Odolf shrank back into himself at the mention of executions, looking more like a scared boy again than a fearless warrior. "If you're going back that way, please don't tell them you saw us," he begged.

"Don't worry," said the mother. "We won't be turning round until we've caught ourselves a nice fat magpike. There's no money in eels and water spiders these days, but a magpike should see us through to winter. Besides," she added, her expression darkening. "Whatever your secret is, it's safe with us. We're no fans of the duchess *or* her cruel punishments." She held up her arm to reveal a missing hand. "That's what

I got for 'stealing' an egg from one of her chickens. Never mind that the daft bird had laid it on *my* doorstep. All I did was pick it up, but that was enough. The thief-catcher wasn't interested in hearing my side of the story—he was too busy sharpening his axe."

"They cut off your hand for a mislaid egg?" Odolf's voice was little more than a worried whisper. "Imagine what they'd do for a stolen belt buckle..."

Emba joined him at the water's edge and laid a comforting hand on his arm. "Shhh," she said. "Don't start imagining that, or you'll never make it to the castle. Think about how brave you were instead, jumping out to face the soldiers just now like a hero. *That's* what you should be focusing on. Even if they did turn out to be river catchers, it was still pretty impressive."

"Really? Well, yes, I suppose it *was* pretty heroic." Odolf stood up straighter and puffed out his chest. "Sorry if I scared you all with my terrifying war cry," he called over to the boat. "Good luck with the magpike-hunting."

The mother waved her arm as the boat continued on

its way, dragging its shiny metal magpike bait through the water behind it.

"How far along the river do you think the soldiers were?" said Odolf, his bravado fading again as the boat disappeared out of sight round the bend. "What if they come this way, looking for a hog chestnut tree to make into an execution block?"

"They wouldn't be able to cut it down if they did," Emba pointed out. "The wood's as tough as steel." She was about to add that the block couldn't be *too* hard in case the executioner's axe bounced straight off again, then changed her mind. The image it conjured up was too frightening. "But if you're worried, we can try going another way, keeping clear of the river altogether."

"Yes," agreed Odolf. "That's a good idea. *I'm* not worried, obviously, but I wouldn't want you to feel scared. Just let me get some water first—being a fearless warrior is thirsty work, you know—and then we'll try cutting through the woods to the road. It might even turn out to be a shortcut."

Emba liked the idea of a shortcut, and so did her

aching legs. She liked the idea of stealing a quick rest too, flopping down on the riverbank next to Odolf as he dipped his upturned hero helmet into the river like a giant cup. But he wasn't the only one to appreciate the delights of a shiny metal helmet gliding through the water...

"Odolf!" Emba screamed, spotting the black and white monster looming up from the depths. "Look out!"

It was too late. Enormous jaws broke through the surface, the magpike's razor teeth clamping round the hero helmet ready to drag it back down to its treasure trove nest.

Odolf let out an un-hero-like scream of surprise, his feet slipping out from underneath him as he toppled into the river after it.

"Let go!" Emba shouted. "Let go of the helmet!"

But Odolf was too shocked—or too stubborn—to listen. His legs thrashed through the water as the magpike swung him from side to side, trying to shake him off.

"Gebb ovv!" he cried through a mouthful of

churned-up river water. River water that went rushing down his throat as the magpike changed tactics and dived downwards, taking Odolf with him.

"Odolf!" Emba cried, willing him to let go. It was only a helmet—they could always find another one from somewhere. She wasn't sure where, exactly, but a replacement helmet would be easier to find than a replacement friend.

The magpike broke the surface again, still trying to shake off its unwanted victim. Odolf spluttered and coughed, water streaming out of his nose and mouth as he gasped for air.

"Help!" he gurgled, his eyes wide with terror. Odolf couldn't let go now, even if he tried, Emba realised with a growing sense of panic. The chin strap had tangled itself round his wrist, anchoring him to his own helmet. If the magpike didn't give up soon and let him go, he'd drown. Emba screamed at the creature in a desperate effort to scare it off, but what chance did she have against a monster like that?

A sudden heat flared inside her chest as she imagined herself swooping down, dragon-like, from the sky, her sharp claws extended. The vision seemed to come from nowhere, filling her with a sudden rush of raw animal energy and focus as she pictured her outstretched talons cutting through the water to pierce the offending magpike's scales. For the briefest of moments she could almost feel the creature bucking and writhing beneath her, as she forced it to relinquish its prize. But then the vision disappeared, as suddenly as it had arrived, and she was herself again: a scared child, watching helpless from the riverbank as her best—and only—friend was pulled down under the water a second time. Except maybe she *wasn't* so helpless after all. The strange vision had given her an idea...

Emba might not have dragon talons at her disposal but Odolf's homemade spear was almost as good. She snatched it up and took aim, waiting for the magpike to resurface. *Come on, come on.* She watched the black and white scales flashing below the water as it twisted and thrashed from side to side.

Come on... Emba's hands trembled as her fingers tightened round the spear. She wasn't sure how much longer Odolf's lungs could last. But then, with a mighty whoosh of water, the magpike came barrelling back up to the surface bringing a flailing, blue-faced Odolf with it.

Emba didn't have long—she knew that. There was no time for sizing up the enemy and taking careful aim. But on the other hand, if she missed, and speared Odolf instead... No, she refused to think about that. She refused to think about anything, letting impulse guide her hand instead, thrusting the spear towards the creature's scaled body.

"Get off my friend, you big brute!" she yelled, as the sharpened tip hit its mark. The magpike rolled over in the water, its mighty jaws snapping open as it let out a low, shrieking cry. Yes! Odolf seized his chance, yanking the helmet clear of the creature's razor teeth and kicking out towards the bank. Emba dragged him wet and spluttering back onto dry land, with a breathless grunt of effort. She wasn't sure who was more relieved—her or Odolf.

Emba hugged him as he coughed and retched, bringing up half a river's worth of water. "No one steals Odolf Bravebuckle's helmet," he gasped, when he could finally speak again. "*Especially* not a fish." He pulled himself free of her arms and reached gingerly back into the water for his spear. The magpike must have shaken it free. "But it's a good job you were there to stop him stealing *me*," he added, turning back to her with a lopsided grin. "Thank you, Emba. If anyone's a hero, it's you."

Chapter 10

The Gathering Clouds of Catastrophe

There was a new, heroic spring to Emba's step after her triumphant river rescue. For a short while, anyway. If she could save Odolf from the magpike, maybe there was hope for their Fred-saving mission too. Maybe the two of them together—her and Odolf—really *did* stand a chance against Necromalcolm. Maybe…

Odolf seemed in surprisingly good spirits too, for someone in his bedraggled state of sogginess. As far as *he* was concerned, his escape from a watery death was further evidence of his belt's protective powers. "I knew it would be alright, really," he said as they marched on. "As long as I had my belt, and you of course, that magpike didn't stand a chance." For all his cheerful swagger he'd been anxious to get going again though, dismissing Emba's suggestion that they should build a quick fire to help dry his clothes.

"There's no time for that," he'd insisted. "I'll dry off soon enough in the sun if we just keep going." His rush to be on his way again was nothing to do with the tree-chopping soldiers who'd been spotted further along the bank, he claimed. Nothing to do with the river catchers' tales of execution blocks and chopped-off hands. "Come on," he said, "the sooner we get to the castle, the sooner we can save Fred."

But Odolf's good spirits soon evaporated, along with the water steaming off his wet clothes. The further into the woods they trudged, the grumpier—and nervier—he became again. His darkening mood seemed to be rubbing off on Emba too, replacing her short-lived burst of triumph and hope with a feeling of gathering gloom. Or maybe it was the darkness of the tree canopy closing in over their heads that was to blame. Or the clouds gathering in the sky above them. One way or another, things were definitely looking darker. And bleaker. And altogether more miserable.

Yes, 'miserable' was the right word for it. The

wearying trudge along the river had been bad enough, but the endless trek through the dark woods was enough to reawaken all Emba's old doubts and fears. What chance did a couple of children have against a powerful necromancer? A magpike was one thing, but Necromalcolm...? And the wearier and weaker she became, the stronger those doubts and fears grew. Perhaps Odolf was feeling the same, Emba thought to herself. Perhaps that accounted for his worried scowl and constant sighs.

"I'm sure the road can't be far away now," he said, sounding decidedly *un*sure. He'd been saying the same thing for what felt like hours, but the road remained as elusive as ever. "Ow!" He rubbed at his elbow, looking pained. His arms were crisscrossed with scratches from stray brambles and branches and, for once, Emba was glad of her thick scales. Her *dragon* scales. The very thought of them—of the dragon blood running through her veins—was enough to reignite the burning feeling inside her. Or maybe it had never gone away. Maybe she'd just grown used to it. But the idea that she'd hatched out of an egg, like a bird, or a lizard, was something else entirely. Emba couldn't see how she'd *ever* grow used to that.

"Ow!" Odolf said again, rubbing at his other elbow. The brambles in this part of the wood were thicker than ever, their tangled strands of thorns encroaching on them from every direction. "This is useless," he said, sighing again. "We're lost."

"No we're not," said Emba, roused from her thoughts of dragons and eggs. "We can't be," she insisted. "We have to get to the castle." *Before Fred suffers a fate so dreadful and calamitous that not even Necromalcolm knows how to spell it.* Emba still didn't know what 'calamitous' meant but it sounded bad.

Odolf sighed some more, flopping down onto a nearby log and flinging his homemade spear onto the ground beside him. "Do *you* know where we are then?" he asked.

"No." Of course she didn't. Emba had never been this far from the cave before.

"Well that makes two of us. Which by my reckoning means we're lost. We should have reached the road ages ago." Odolf leapt up in fright as a spider ran over his leg. But instead of laughing when he saw what it was, he scowled. "Look at me," he said. "Jumping at the smallest things. This was a bad idea. In fact, this whole trip's been a bad idea from start to finish." He took off his helmet and threw it against a tree, cursing under his breath. "I should never have let you talk me into it. This is all your fault," he hissed.

Emba stared at him in surprise. Odolf could be pretty annoying at times—make that *very* annoying, not to mention vain and boastful and full of nonsense—but he was never angry. Or if he was, he never took it out on her.

"*My* fault?" she spluttered, the burning in her belly and throat growing hotter than ever. "I'm not the one who told Necromalcolm's beardy man where to find me. I'm not the one who gave him directions to the cave so that he could come back with his evil beardy friend and steal Fred away in the middle of the night."

"How do you know whether his friend had a beard? I thought you said you were asleep. Maybe if you hadn't been so busy snoring, you'd have been able to stop them."

"Me? I don't snore," Emba said. "*You're* the one who snores. I heard you last week when I was out early, fetching water. Your whole tree was shaking." *Just like Fred*, she thought. *Fred could have brought down an entire forest with her snores.* "And I'm only guessing about the beard. You heard what Fred said yesterday—every man over the age of twenty has a beard." Yes, Fred knew all about beards, just like she knew about everything else. *She* wouldn't have got them lost in the middle of the woods, like Odolf had. *But then again*, thought Emba with a pang of guilt, *Odolf's not the one who lost my leather pouch, allowing Necromalcolm to spy on me in his scrying bowl. If only I'd kept it round my neck like I was supposed to, there wouldn't have* been *any bearded men sniffing round the woods asking questions about dragon girls in the first place. And we wouldn't be here now, feeling lost and angry at each other. If anyone's to blame, it's me.*

Emba picked up Odolf's fallen helmet and handed it back to him. "I'm sorry," she said, the heat in her belly cooling along with her temper. "You're right. It's my fault we're in this mess. *I'm* the reason they took Fred. Maybe we need a rest and something to eat—things will seem better then, I'm sure."

"And maybe the road will magically appear through the trees and Fred will defeat Necromalcolm and we'll all live happily ever after," said Odolf bitterly. "I don't see how a bit of food's going to change anything. We'll still be lost."

"What if the bit of food was honey and quince scones?"

Odolf's frown softened. "Honey and quince scones?" he repeated wistfully. "But where would we get them in the middle of the woods?"

"From my bag, of course," said Emba. "You didn't think I'd set off on a daring rescue mission without scones, did you?" She sat down beside him and slipped her goatskin bag off her shoulder. "At least, they *were* scones," she added, peering inside. Long hours of repeated jostling against her flask and blanket had *not* been kind to them. "What about a handful of honey and quince crumbly lumps with added furry bits? How does that sound?"

Odolf was grinning now, much to Emba's relief. Things were bad enough as it was, without the pair of them falling out. "That sounds perfect," he said. "Furry bits are my favourite."

Emba was right. Things *did* seem better once they'd had a proper rest and something to eat. The foraged nuts and berries they'd had along the way had done little to fill their bellies, and even less to soothe their anxious minds. But, as Fred always said, there were no problems in life that couldn't be made better by honey and quince scones. Did that include finding out you were an unwanted human hatchling, Emba wondered? What about middle-of-the-night kidnappings and blood-seeking necromancers?

None of those problems had gone away, but the scones must have worked their magic on Emba and Odolf all the same. There was no denying the world looked a little brighter again *after* their slightly damp-bottomed picnic of scones than it had before. Apart from the ever-darkening clouds overhead, that was. And the pulsing red crack in the sky...

"Look, Odolf, it's back," Emba cried.

Odolf followed her gaze, staring up into the heavens as he licked the last few scone crumbs from round his mouth. "What's back? I can't see where you're pointing. Is it the dragon?"

"No, the crack," said Emba. "The crack in the sky. Can't you see it?"

But maybe Odolf had a point. Perhaps the two went hand in hand. If the crack was back, the dragon might not be far behind. The thought filled Emba with a hot shivery dread... dread and something else. Something that felt oddly like longing... almost as if she *wanted* a dragon to come swooping down out of the sky and carry her away from all her worries.

No, that was crazy. What Emba *really* wanted was to find a way out of these never-ending woods, rescue Fred from the castle without getting her blood drained in the process, and go back to her nice, Necromalcolm-free, *dragon*-free life. The actual rescuing part of the plan was still a bit hazy—Emba Oak wasn't exactly an expert when it came to rescuing hermits from deep, dark dungeons—but hopefully things would be clearer once they got there. Once they knew what they were up against.

"The only thing *I* can see is clouds," said Odolf. "And I don't like the look of them very much either. We're going to get soaked. My undergarments have only just dried off after the river."

But Emba barely heard him. She was too busy listening to the sudden rush of air that came swooping down over the treetops. To the flapping, beating noise above her head. Her belly flickered with heat, her throat burning again as she stared up into the empty sky.

"You're here," she whispered, the words forming in her mouth of their own accord. There was nothing to see this time—no enormous boned wings, no sad milky eyes or silvered dinner-plate scales and yet... and yet Emba knew.

You're here, came the reply, like an echo, carried through the air in the rhythmic beating of invisible wings. *You're here, you're here, you're here...* or maybe it was *beware. Beware, beware, beware...*

"It's happening again, isn't it?" came a voice from

somewhere far away. Not a dragon voice, though. It was too high and squeaky for that. "I wish *I* could see it too."

And then suddenly the voice—*Odolf's* voice—was right there in her ear, and the rush of air was simply the wind, swirling through the trees, pushing the ever-darkening clouds on across the sky.

Emba blinked in surprise, staring about her as if she'd forgotten where she was. Perhaps she had, for a moment. But there was her goatskin bag, slumped against the damp log. There was Odolf's sharpened spear. And there was Odolf himself, staring at her with an odd expression on his face. "Can you see me?" he asked.

Emba blinked again. "What do you mean? Of course I can see you. Why are you looking at me like that?"

"It was your eyes," said Odolf. "The black bits in the middle. They went all strange and out-of-shape... Sort of long and pointy, instead of round. Please don't do that again—it was really creepy."

"I didn't *do* anything," said Emba. "It must have been something to do with the dragon." She glanced back up into the sky, but there was still nothing there. No dark wing-spread shape silhouetted against the sun (and no sun, come to that, either). No long, pointed tail whipping through the heavens. No sign that she hadn't imagined the whole thing. Even the crack was gone… if it had ever been there in the first place.

Not that the sky was *completely* empty. Far from it. In fact, the longer she stood there, gazing up in confusion, the heavier the clouds seemed to grow. It was only a matter of time before they—

There was a mighty roar. Not a dragon roar, though. A sudden roar of water pelting down from the sky like Wishman's Waterfall, running straight off the trees onto their heads. "I told you we'd get soaked," Odolf squealed, scrambling to put his helmet back on.

Emba reached inside her bag for her blanket and draped it round her shoulders to try and keep the worst of the rain off. But she was fighting a losing battle on that score.

"Come on," said Odolf, water already streaming off the end of his nose. "I think that's our cue to get moving again. I've had enough of being lost. We're going to find that road if it's the last thing we do."

And there, just two more arguments and one soaking later, it was! It wasn't a particularly impressive road, but Emba had never been so pleased to see a muddy-puddled, horse-dung-dolloped thoroughfare in her life. She could have got down on her hands and knees and kissed it, if it wasn't for all the muddy puddles and horse dung. As it was, she settled for a friendly thump of Odolf's arm, and a very relieved smile. It felt like they were finally on their way. Now all they needed to do was flag down a passing hay wagon—preferably one headed for the castle—and save Fred.

Chapter 11

The Fickle Finger of Fortune

"How much further now?" asked Emba, shivering in her wet blanket.

Odolf yawned. "About three hundred yards less than the last time you asked."

Emba's hopes for a passing cart had dwindled with the dying daylight. Her dreams of a nice cosy ride— and a well-earned rest from the endless trudging—had dribbled away to nothing in the cold evening drizzle. The castle, along with her daring rescue, would have to wait until tomorrow. All she wanted now was somewhere warm and dry to spend the night. Somewhere exactly like the old hilltop shepherd's hut Odolf had taken shelter in during his great escape, two years earlier. That's where they were headed for. But either the hill (and the shepherd hut) had grown legs and moved, or Odolf had misremembered quite how far away it was. Not that he was admitting to anything of the sort.

"I thought you said the turning was right after the ford," she grumbled. "That was *miles* back. Are you sure you know where you're going?"

"Of course I do," Odolf assured her. Emba didn't feel remotely assured though. He'd been promising that they were nearly there for the last hour or so. "It should be coming up on the left, any minute now. At least I *think* it was on the left."

They trudged on in silence, save for the wet splat of their feet against the muddy track and the loud rumbling of Emba's stomach. Their honey and quince scones felt like a lifetime ago.

"What about trying that old barn instead?" suggested Emba, pointing through the gathering gloom. "We could bed down there for the night, with the animals. I'm sure the farmer wouldn't mind." She was thinking of the farmer who'd come to the cave a few summers ago—a kind, gentle giant of a man who wanted the

Tome of Terrible Tomorrows to tell him how to save his sickly son.

"I'm not so sure about that," said Odolf. "The last time I asked a farmer for anything, he chased me out the field with a pitchfork. I only wanted an apple." He shook his head. "I say we keep going."

But Emba wasn't sure how much longer she *could* keep going for. "There aren't any lights coming from the farmhouse—they're probably in bed already." She thought longingly of her own bed, back at the cave. Her lumpy pillow and scratchy mattress had never seemed warmer or cosier. "We could sneak into the barn *without* asking, if you'd rather."

"No thank you," said Odolf. "I've had enough pitchforks in my bottom to last a lifetime."

"What? It was only the one, surely?" Getting attacked with pitchforks didn't seem like the sort of thing Odolf made a habit of.

"Trust me, one was more than enough," he said, shuddering at the memory. "Come on, let's keep going. The hut can't be much further now."

"What if there's already a shepherd inside?" asked

Emba, staring longingly at the barn. "What if we get there and there's no room for us to sleep?"

Odolf's pace slowed. "I'm sure it'll be fine," he said, uncertainly.

"And what if the shepherd's really grumpy that we've woken him up, and chases us out with his shepherd's crook?" Emba didn't think that was particularly likely—the only shepherds she'd met were gentle, quiet-mannered souls—but the call of the warm dry barn was too loud to ignore. The thought of traipsing on through the cold, wet night in search of Odolf's elusive hut filled her with a shivering, soggy misery. "If you don't like pitchforks in your bottom, you won't like crooks either. I say we find shelter while we can. Without some proper rest we'll be no good for anything tomorrow. We owe it to Fred to get some sleep," she added.

There. Surely he couldn't argue with *that*. Bringing Fred into it was a bit of a low trick, but it was true. How were they supposed to take on an evil, blood-draining necromancer, not to mention the duchess's guards, if they couldn't even keep their eyes open?

"I suppose…" Odolf was wavering now. She could hear it in his voice.

Emba pressed home her advantage. "And if we're *really* lucky there might be some spare apples for dinner," she said. Did farmers store apples in barns? Or was that just hay? "Mm, nice crunchy apples." Her stomach rumbled louder than ever.

Odolf came to a complete standstill. "Do you really think so?"

"There's only one way to find out…"

They crept up to the barn door, keeping firmly to the shadows, and peered inside. It was dark but inviting; a warm, fuggy smell of animals hanging heavy in the air. *Mm, yes*, thought Emba, breathing it in. It smelt of sweat and muck and sleep. Sweet, sweet sleep.

"What do you think?" she asked, squinting into the gloom. There were no signs of any wildly-waving pitchforks—that was a good start. No sign of any cross farmers. It was just them, the animals, and a nice warm stack of hay.

"It *seems* safe enough," agreed Odolf.

"Of course it's safe," Emba told him. "Besides, you've

got your magic belt to protect you. Not to mention your natural heroism. Surely Odolf Bravebuckle isn't scared of a few cows and horses?"

"I didn't say I was scared. I just wanted to check it was safe for you, that's all." Odolf paused, peering into the darkness and sniffing the air. "I can't see any apples though."

Emba's stomach rumbled again in sympathy. If only they hadn't polished off all the scones earlier. If only she'd thought to pack some more provisions. But food would have to wait a little longer. "We'll find some first thing tomorrow, I promise. And if not apples, then something even tastier." Maybe she could persuade Odolf to catch them a rabbit for breakfast. She was getting rather good at persuading.

"Alright," he agreed, taking off his helmet and propping his wooden spear up against the wall. He undid his belt, tucking it inside his upturned helmet for safekeeping, before flopping down into the hay. "I could do with some shut-eye. But we need to be up and away nice and early. I don't want to be here when the farmer comes tomorrow."

"It's a deal." Emba spread her wet blanket out to dry, took off her bag and burrowed down into the hay beside him. "The best thing we can do now is close our eyes and get a good night's sleep," she murmured, borrowing Fred's advice from the night before. Was it really only a day ago? "Everything will seem better in the morning, you'll see."

If only Fred was there now to share her advice in person. To give Emba her warm goat's milk and tuck her into bed. To sing her into safety with her nightly lullaby-charm. But there'd be no milk tonight—not unless there was a willing goat there in the barn. And Emba was far too tired to do battle with an *un*willing one, especially in the dark. Imagine what would happen if she tried milking it by its tail! But there was nothing to stop her from singing…

Keep me safe in sleep tonight,
From murderous tooth and claw,
From flashing blade and bloodied sword
And monsters bathed in gore…"

"Give it a rest," came an irritated murmur. "Some of us are trying to sleep."

No, there was nothing at all to stop her singing—apart from Odolf and a grumpy kick in the shin.

Both of the dragons were back again that night—soaring and chasing through her dreams, calling for her to hurry up and get the horse out of there. Wait a minute, that wasn't part of her dream... Emba struggled back into wakefulness, her body rigid with fear. A pair of lights bobbed in the darkness before her, like giant fireflies. Like lanterns. *Necromalcolm's henchmen are in the cave*, she thought, her heart pounding hot and fast inside her chest. *They've come back for me.* And then she remembered she wasn't *in* the cave. And whoever was in the barn, it wasn't *her* they were stealing away with, it was a horse. *Hurry up and get the horse out of here.* Yes, now that she was properly awake, Emba was certain that's what she'd heard. And she was equally certain it hadn't been the farmer speaking.

"Odolf," she whispered. "Wake up."

There was a soft moan and a wriggling sound—the

sound of someone turning over in their sleep—and then the snoring started. Loud snoring.

"'Ere, what was that?" said a voice.

Emba closed her eyes against the bright light that came bobbing towards them. She thought of her scaring-off stone, tucked away again inside her goatskin bag for safe-keeping. *Curses*. She thought of Odolf's sharpened stick, propped up against the barn wall out of reach. She thought of the protective lullaby charm she never finished singing... The only defence she had left was the leather pouch of toenail shards round her neck, so she clutched onto that in the vain hope that it would help. Maybe it would render her invisible to lantern-bearing horse thieves as well as Necromalcolm's scrying bowl...

"Must be the pigs," came a second voice, lower and gruffer than the first. "Smells like pigs to me."

It was working! Emba squeezed her leather pouch even tighter, hardly daring to breathe. Not that anyone would hear over Odolf's pig-like grunts and snorts.

"'Old on, there's somethin' there," said the first voice.

Oh no, they've seen us. Emba forced herself to

open her eyes. Forced herself to look. A heavy-set face with dark shaggy eyebrows and a tangled black beard flickered into light as the man lifted his lantern, leaning in for a closer inspection. *Please don't hurt us.*

Tanglebeard's eyes glimmered. "Somethin' shiny," he said.

It must be the sweat on my face glinting in the lantern's glare, Emba thought. But she was wrong.

"It looks like some kind of 'elmet to me," said Tanglebeard. He bent down, dropping away into darkness. "It *is!* It's a blimmin' 'elmet!"

"Well don't jus' stand there gawpin' at it," growled the second voice. "Grab it and go. Come on, 'urry up, before someone catches us."

No, no, no! Not Odolf's hero helmet! Emba's insides began to burn again, as paralysed fear gave way to paralysed anger. But what could she do? The man was three times her size and the only weapon she had to hand was a shard of toenail.

"Wait," said Tanglebeard. "Look! There's somethin' inside it! A belt!" There was a soft whistling sound like someone sucking air in through their teeth.

"A proper fancy one too, with a dragon buckle. Look at that workmanship! That's worth more than two 'orses put together, I reckon."

Not his belt! No! You can't take that. "Pssst, Odolf," Emba hissed again, "wake up." She reached out her hand to shake him.

"Aagghhh!" came a sudden cry. A loud, fearful sort of cry. The lantern swung wildly as Tanglebeard stumbled backwards. "It's a snake!" he yelled. There was a loud clunking sound, like something hard and metal hitting the floor.

Emba whipped her hand back as if she'd been stung—as if she'd been *bitten*—her heart hammering faster than ever. She gulped. *A snake?* Just when she thought things couldn't get any worse... If there was one thing Emba Oak hated, it was snakes. And big hairy spiders. And lice. And turnip stew. And snare trees. And horrible helmet-snatching magpikes. Actually, there were quite a lot of things Emba Oak hated. Not to mention hermit-stealing necromancers. She *really* hated them. But, necromancers aside, snakes were right up there at the top of her list.

Chapter 12

The Fearsome Fangs of Misfortune

Please don't let it bite me. Emba had been bitten before—a nasty nip on the finger from a baby allum snake hiding inside a hole in the rocks. But Fred had been there to suck out the poison and cool the throbbing pain with a soothing balm. To dry Emba's tears and tell her everything was going to be alright. There was no Fred to help this time, if the snake chose to attack. No one to stop the poison coursing through Emba's body, all the way to her heart…

She lay perfectly still, ears strained for the tell-tale hiss of the snake slithering through the hay towards her. But all she could hear was Odolf—still snoring away, as oblivious as ever—and the frantic beating inside her own chest.

"A snake?" called the second man. "What kind of snake?"

"'Ow should I know what kind of snake it is?" came the reply. "A ruddy big one, that's for sure. It was wrigglin' round in the hay, all scaly and 'orrible-lookin'. It was 'issin' too—didn't you 'ear it?"

Something rustled nearby and it took every ounce of Emba's self-control not to scream. Not to fling herself out of the way and make a run for it. But snakes didn't like sudden movements, that's what Fred had told her. She said they only bit people when they were scared. Besides, it might not have been the snake rustling in the hay. It might have been Odolf, fidgeting in his sleep.

Perhaps I should warn him, she thought, *in case he wakes up and panics.*

"*Pssst,*" she hissed.

Odolf carried on snoring.

Emba tried again, a little louder this time. "*Pssssssst.*"

"There!" cried Tanglebeard. "There it goes again. I can't see it though. Watch out, it could be anywhere by now."

Wait a minute, thought Emba. *That wasn't the snake, it was me!*

"Well don't jus' stand there, then," called the second man. "We don't want it scaring the 'orse. Come on, let's get outta 'ere."

The intruders headed for the door, taking their lights and their noise with them, the stolen horse whinnying in protest. But then, with a final clattering curse from Tanglebeard—something about stubbing his toe on a sharp wooden stick someone had left by the wall— they were gone, plunging the barn back into darkness. It took another panicked moment or two for Emba to realise what had happened. There never *was* a snake, was there? It must have been her arm that the man had seen, moving through the hay.

All scaly and horrible-looking? she thought, feeling relieved and insulted at the same time. *Charming!*

Odolf let out a sudden snort beside her. "What was that?" he whispered. "I thought I heard something."

"That'll be the horse thieves," said Emba, "escaping from the snake."

"Horse thieves?" repeated Odolf, like an echo.

"Snake?"

"Don't worry, the snake was a false alarm. It turned out it was only—" Emba broke off in surprise. The clouds covering the moon must have shifted. A thin, silvery light shone in through the hole in the roof. Just enough light to see Odolf reaching out of the hay and running his hands along the floor. "What are you doing?" she asked.

"Looking for my helmet and belt," he said, as if the answer was obvious.

"Oh." Emba had forgotten all about them in the snake drama. "Oh dear. The thing is, Odolf, I think one of the thieves might have taken..." She could hardly bring herself to say it. He'd probably go charging off after them and end up in a fight. A fight he had little chance of winning, hero training or no hero training. Battling imaginary enemies in the woods was one thing, but tackling real-life thieves, with real-life fists and knives was something else again.

"They were just here, I don't understand." Odolf was down on his hands and knees now, crawling across the barn floor.

"I'm really sorry," said Emba, following after him. "I tried waking you up, but—"

"My helmet!" he cried. "Thank goodness for that... wait a minute, where's my belt? I left it tucked inside, I know I did."

Emba remembered the loud metallic clunk she'd heard earlier, when the thief spotted the so-called snake. That must have been Odolf's helmet hitting the barn floor. But what about the belt? Had the thief already threaded it round his own waist? "The horse thief must have taken it," she said. "I heard him saying how fancy the dragon buckle was. How it was worth two horses put together."

"No," muttered Odolf, still scrabbling round on the floor. "It's got to be here. It *has* to be. I'm Odolf Bravebuckle. That's who I am."

"I'm sure we can get you another buckle from somewhere, once we've saved Fred," Emba told him. "Or you could change your name to Odolf Bravehelmet. Yes," she lied. "Odolf Bravehelmet sounds even better. Even braver." No it didn't, it sounded ridiculous. "Or Odolf Bravespear? I don't think the thieves took that—in fact, one of them stubbed his toe on it on the way out."

Odolf didn't answer. Perhaps he hadn't heard. He was still muttering to himself. Still searching. "It can't have gone. It must be here somewhere." It was heartbreaking to watch. Heartbreaking to hear. "Have you got your scaring-off stone?" he asked at last.

"Yes," said Emba. "Of course." She felt around inside her goatskin bag for her trusty sharpened flint. "Here we go." She was about to hand it over when she thought better of it. "What do you need it for? You're not going to do anything silly are you?" *Like chasing after them.*

Odolf thought for a moment. "That depends what you mean by 'silly'. Does starting a fire in a barn full of hay count? I thought with your stone and my helmet, I could—"

"Yes," said Emba, cutting him off short. "That sounds *really* silly." She imagined Odolf rubbing her stone against the metal of his helmet to make a few sparks… and then a stray spark catching on the hay… and then *whoof,* the whole place going up in flames. *Hmm, fire…* she thought. *Beautiful burning fire…* Emba shook her head. *What? No, not beautiful. Deadly. Where on earth had that come from?*

"Are you alright?" asked Odolf. "Your eyes went all strange again then. They were sort of glowing in the dark. And the black bits in the middle started flickering and changing shape."

But it wasn't Emba's eyes that felt strange and flickering. It was the hot tongues of heat dancing in her stomach. Why did that keep happening?

"Emba?" Odolf was still waiting for an answer.

"Yes, I'm fine," she said, dragging her mind back to the here and now. To Odolf's ridiculous plan. "And I'm sorry, but you're not using my stone to start a fire in here. It's too dangerous."

"Only a little one," he said. "Just so I can see better. Just enough light to find my belt… I have to find it, Emba. I *have* to… otherwise…" He broke off, sobbing. "Otherwise… I w-won't be m-me anymore."

"Oh Odolf." Emba reached for him in the gloom, wrapping her arms round his skinny shoulders. She could feel him shaking. "You'll still be you, even without your belt. You'll still be the same brave, funny, slightly annoying person you always were. A stolen buckle can't change that."

"It changes *everything*," he insisted. "I was just a scared, skinny boy before I put that buckle on. I wouldn't say 'boo' to a goose."

"That's alright," said Emba. "Nor would I. Geese can be pretty mean and aggressive."

Odolf wasn't having any of it though. "You know what I mean. I was a proper scaredy-cat, *that's* what I'm trying to tell you. I used to jump at my own shadow. But from the moment I picked up that buckle and threaded it onto my belt I became a new man. Well, a new boy, anyway. I felt like I could do anything. Could *be* anything. I felt invincible."

You can't have felt that *invincible*, thought Emba. *You still ran away when you heard your master coming.*

"It felt like destiny was calling me," Odolf went on. "Calling me to step up and take my place in the world. To be a hero. And then when I met you and Fred, and heard about the Final Prophecy in the Tome of Terrible Tomorrows, that's when I knew for sure.

That's when I said goodbye to the old Odolf once and for all. That's when I became Odolf Bravebuckle, a hero forged in fiercest flame, come to save the kingdom from being torn in two. How am I supposed to save anything without my belt though? Without its protective magic?"

Emba squeezed him even tighter. "You've still got your helmet," she said. "Maybe *that's* magic too."

"No it's not. It's just a helmet. And a dented helmet at that, by the feel of it."

"Ah yes," said Emba. "I think the thief might have dropped it. But that's alright—maybe the dent makes it *more* magical. And you've still got me. That's got to count for something. I'd swap a magic belt for a friend, any day."

Odolf sniffed.

"Plus you've got Fred as well. She thinks you're pretty great too—with or without your buckle. And right now Fred needs you to pull yourself together and get on with saving her. Come on, Odolf, this is your chance to *really* be a hero."

Odolf pulled away. "I'm sorry, Emba," he said

quietly. "I can't do this."

"Can't do what? The hugging? I agree, it did feel a bit weird, didn't it? How about a friendly punch in the arm instead?"

"No," said Odolf. "I mean *this*. This quest of yours. I'm not a brave hero—I never was. I see that now. I can't go to the castle with you—not without my belt to protect me. Not that it would do any good anyway. You know what the prophecy said:

Bonds shall break and shackles shake
Before the hero's ire.

There's no way I can break Fred's bonds and shake her shackles without my iron buckle."

"We're only guessing about the 'ire' bit," Emba pointed out. "It might *not* be short for iron. It might be nothing to do with your belt."

"Exactly," said Odolf. "We don't really know what *any* of it means. Fred might not even *be* at Gravethorn Castle. I could be risking my life for nothing."

Emba remembered the flapping beat of dragon wings in the woods. *Beware, beware, beware.* Maybe it really *had* been a warning after all. Beware of the barn. Beware of the thieves. Beware of everything falling to pieces before you're even halfway through your journey.

"You don't know what the duchess is like," Odolf went on. His voice sounded very small all of a sudden. Small and scared. "She'll have me strung up by my feet as a thief quicker than I can say 'sorry, I didn't mean to take it.'"

"That doesn't sound so bad," said Emba, trying not to panic. Trying to think what to say for the best. There was no way she could save Fred on her own. "I mean, it doesn't sound *great*, but I'll be there to unstring you again."

"No, you don't understand. She'll have me strung up by my feet *after* she's chopped off my hands for stealing." Odolf sniffed. "Though I don't suppose I'll care too much if she's already chopped off my head."

"Your head too? There won't be much of you left at this rate," joked Emba. Not that the chopping-off of body parts was a laughing matter.

For a moment, she thought it had worked though. She thought Odolf was laughing. Shaking with laughter in fact. But it was misery coursing through his body, not merriment. "I don't want to lose my head," he sobbed. "Or my hands. And I *hate* being upside-down. It makes me feel dizzy. I'm sorry, Emba. I'm sorry for being such a coward. But I can't do it. I really mean it this time. From now on, you're on your own. I'm going home."

Chapter 13

The Lonely Road to Ruin

All the best stories and adventures have a low, despairing point somewhere round the middle—a point where things look so bleak for the hero that they feel like giving up. Emba Oak had listened to enough nail-biting narrations round the fire to know that. But *knowing* it didn't make *living* through it any easier. Odolf had already given up, and Emba had never felt less heroic in her life. She wished she could skip straight through the miserable middle to the exciting end, where everything somehow worked out for the best, without anyone getting their head chopped off *or* having their blood drained by an evil necromancer. But what if her story *didn't* work out for the best? What if hers was the exception to the rule, and it all ended in misery and misfortune?

Watching Odolf heading off into the pre-dawn gloom, without her, had been the lowest point of all. It took every bit of self-restraint not to run after him. Not to follow him home to the cave and wait for a better, safer plan to reveal itself. Emba had never been this far from home before, and the idea of carrying on alone, into the unknown, filled her with dread. But then she remembered the calamitous fate that would befall Fred if she gave up now, and knew it wasn't an option. Instead she wrapped her still-damp blanket round her shoulders, set her face towards the castle and started walking.

According to Odolf's detailed directions, she should reach the Pool of Perilous Perception by noon. And from there it was a mere twelve-hour uphill slog through dangerous bear country until she reached the outskirts of Gravethorn. "Nothing to it," she said out loud, clutching her scaring-off stone tight inside her fist. "I'll be back home with Fred before I know it."

Things seemed a *little* brighter once the sun was up. At least Emba could see the cold muddy puddles before she stepped in them now. Her feet were slightly drier for it, but they still ached after all her walking the day before. The ache in her heart was as heavy as ever too. In fact, it was twice as heavy, with Fred *and* Odolf gone. And the more Emba thought about it, the heavier her heart grew. As for the gnawing ache of hunger in her stomach, that was getting worse with every woeful step.

"How much further now?" she asked a scruffy old scarecrow along the way. "About three hundred yards less than the last time I asked?" But the scarecrow stared blindly off into the distance, his tattered coat flapping in the morning breeze. His stuffed-headed silence only made her miss Odolf more. *Why did he have to leave me? I thought we were friends.*

Emba stopped off for a breakfast drink at the first stream she came to, refilling her sheep's bladder with water for the day. Breakfast *food* was harder to come by though. She had to make do with an old turnip she found lying in the road. It must've fallen off the back of a passing cart—and quite some while ago too, judging by the state of it. Turnips were disgusting enough at the best of times, but a rotting *raw* turnip took disgusting to a whole new level. Every single bite was an ordeal.

Mmm, this half-crunchy, half-mushy honey and quince scone is delicious, she told herself, trying to trick her mind—and her mouth—into enjoying it. But her mind wasn't as easily fooled as all that. And neither was her mouth. *That's not a scone, you fool, it's a disgusting rotten turnip*—that's what her mouth would have said in reply, if it wasn't too full of disgusting rotten turnip to speak. Emba needed to keep her strength up though, so she forced down as much as she could and put the rest in her bag for later. If she didn't manage to flag down a cart, it was going to be a long, hungry day.

Carts were few and far between along that particular stretch of road though. The sun was well over the trees by the time the first one came trundling along with its clattering load of barrels. The driver—a gnarly old man with a beard down to his waist—nodded in response to Emba's wild waving, but showed no sign of slowing down.

"Hello there," she called up as he drew level with her. "I'm trying to get to Gravethorn Castle. Any chance of a ride?" But the man shook his head, whipping the horse on without so much as a word. *Charming*.

Emba missed the next cart altogether, thanks to an ill-timed wee stop behind a bush. By the time she made it back to the road it was too late—it was already rumbling off up the hill without her. "Wait, come back!" she shouted, chasing after it. "Please—I have to get to Gravethorn. It's a matter of life and death." But all she got for her efforts was a stitch in her side and a face-first tumble into a fresh dollop of horse poo, which did very little to improve her mood.

She'd almost given up hope by the time the third cart came along. What was the point? But Emba Oak had never been one to admit defeat, so she stepped into the middle of the road as the cart drew near and waved the end of her blanket in the air, to get it to stop. *Third time lucky*.

"Woah," cried the driver, pulling sharply on the reins. "Watch out there!" He was a round, red-faced man, with wild scarecrow-like hair poking out from underneath his holey hat. Hopefully he'd have more to say for himself than the scarecrow had though. Something like, "of course you can have a lift to the castle. It would be my pleasure. I've got some bread and cheese too if you're hungry." And were those chickens Emba could hear in the back? Maybe he'd have an egg going spare as well, and a pan to cook it in...

Oh yes, she thought, licking her lips at the very idea. *That'll do nicely.*

"Thank you for stopping," she called up to him. (Not that she'd given him much choice in the matter.) "I'm trying to get to Gravethorn Castle. I was hoping I might be able to get a lift with you. Please," she added, with what she hoped was an encouraging kind of smile.

And, for one wonderful moment, it looked like it had worked. Like her luck had finally, *finally* begun to change.

The man smiled back at her, revealing a sprinkling of crooked brown teeth. "To the castle, you say? Go on then, up you hop. As long as you don't mind sharing with the chickens." He didn't mention anything about bread and cheese, or spare eggs, but a lift was an excellent start. He even climbed down into the road to help her up. But then her blanket slipped as she reached for the side of the cart, and his attitude changed altogether. The smile withered on his lips and his voice grew mean and snarly. "Oh no you don't," he said, catching hold of her blanket and yanking it away. "Look at you! You're all scaly like a snake! You'll frighten the chickens half to death."

"Please," Emba begged him. "It's not my fault. I can't help the way I look. I won't hurt them though, I swear."

The man's lip curled up in disgust—or maybe it was fear. "I've never seen anything like it," he muttered to himself. "That's unnatural, that is. *You're* unnatural." He hurled Emba aside, sending her sprawling into a nearby puddle. "Go on, off you go. Scram! Filthy witch-child," he hissed.

"I'm not a witch-child," said Emba. "I'm a…" *A what, exactly? A hatchling? An unwanted dragon castoff? A friendless freak with nothing but a rotten turnip to my name? Yes, that's me.*

There weren't many carts after that—not that Emba could face asking again, anyway. And when a rich-looking young man on horseback stopped to ask her for directions to the Pool of Perilous Perception, she was too miserable to even reply. She simply shrugged her shoulders and carried on walking. Thinking about the pool made her feel even sadder. It reminded her of Odolf. Of what he'd told her before they went their separate ways:

"Be careful when you get to the pool," he'd warned her. "If you stare deep into its waters, you'll either see your one true desire reflected there or your one true fear. The problem is, you won't know which one it is. They say folk have been driven mad by the visions they've seen, chasing off after dreams that turned out to be their worst nightmares."

"What about you?" Emba had asked. "Have you tried it?"

Odolf nodded. "After I ran away from the castle," he said. "I thought maybe if I knew what my true desire was it might help me decide what to do next."

"And did it?"

"Yes," he said. "At least that's what I thought at the time. I saw a vision of myself as a great warrior. A hero. I already knew what my greatest fear was—a grizzly end at the hands of the duchess—so the reflection had to be my one true desire. And not just my desire, either, but my destiny. Only now... now that the time's finally come for me to step up and become the hero I always wanted to be, I'm too scared. I guess it must have been my one true fear all along."

Emba didn't need to look into any pools to know what *her* greatest fear was. The idea of losing Fred forever was too terrifying to even imagine. And right now, *saving* Fred was her only desire. Well, saving Fred and finding something else to eat. Something other than rotten turnip. *Forget about pools of perception*, she thought, *I'd rather visit a pool of pleasant porridge any day. Or a pool of pear pudding.* As for the perilous part—Emba Oak had enough of that in her life already, thank you very much. At least she *thought* she did. But, as with all the best stories and adventures, there was plenty more peril to come.

Chapter 14

The Chicken Leg of Lost Hope

Despite her reservations, Emba was pleased to see the Pool of Perilous Perception when she finally arrived, just after midday. It meant the first part of her long solo journey lay behind her now. It meant she was one step closer to finding Fred than she had been before. And it meant it was lunchtime.

She sat down under a tree, well away from the water's edge, and fished around in her bag for the remainder of her turnip. Her hopes that a tastier alternative might present itself on the way—some fruit or wild ears of wheat, or even a non-rotten turnip—had come to nothing. But the gnawing pangs of hunger in her stomach were growing too strong to ignore, so the turnip would have to do. At least she had plenty of water left to wash it down with.

Emba held her nose, stealing herself for the full horror of her first bite. Yes, the first bite was definitely the worst. Apart from the second bite, that was. And the third and the fourth... She shut her eyes in the vain hope that not being able to see or smell it would somehow keep her from tasting it too. *After three. One.... Two...*

"Excuse me?"

Emba was saved from a fate worse than hunger by a rich, plummy voice coming from somewhere overhead. A strangely familiar-sounding voice... She opened her eyes and looked up to see the rich-looking young man with the horse, who'd asked her for directions to the pool earlier that morning. Not that he was on his horse now, though. He was perched on a low-hanging branch above her head, clutching what looked like a leg of chicken.

"Hello again," she said, her mouth watering at the thought of scrumptious, succulent meat just a few feet away. "Sorry, I didn't see you up there. And sorry I couldn't help you earlier when you asked for directions. I was having a bit of a crisis." *My whole life is one big crisis right now.* She quickly pulled her blanket back up over her shoulders, before *he* could accuse her of being a witch-child too.

The man squinted back at her. "Oh," he said, sounding surprised. "Was that you? I'm afraid my eyesight's not very good."

Emba relaxed a little. Perhaps he wouldn't be able to see her scales anyway then. "But you found your way here, alright," she said.

The man nodded. "Yes, for all the good it's done me. I'm starting to think the Pool of Perilous Perception was a mistake. The longer I stay here the more confused I get, but I can't quite drag myself away. I keep thinking if I have another look it might be clearer this time. That this time I'll know for sure."

"Know what?" asked Emba. Maybe if she kept him talking, he might offer her a bite of his chicken.

The man sighed, flinging the delicious-looking leg away, untouched. "It's no good. I can't eat at a time like this. Father says I need to find myself a wife," he explained. "Otherwise he'll find one for me. Only

I'm not sure if I'm ready for marriage yet. Perhaps I'd rather be a soldier. Or a sailor. Or a priest…"

Emba was too busy scrabbling through the undergrowth for the discarded chicken to answer at first. *There! Got it!* It was a bit grassier than she'd have liked, but nothing that couldn't be wiped off on the hem of her tunic.

"Oh," she mumbled back, through a mouthful of utter deliciousness. "That's heavenly. I mean, horrible," she added quickly. "Horribly tricky. What exactly did you see when you looked into the pool?"

The man sighed again. "I *think* I saw a woman in a white apron, surrounded by children. *Lots* of children. Though it was all a bit blurry if I'm honest. And I *think* I saw myself standing behind her, holding a screaming baby. Does that mean a family's what I really want, deep down, or was that my deepest fear being reflected back at me? How am I supposed to tell? Oh it's all so complicated. Maybe if you were to look into the pool with me, and make sure that really *is* what I'm looking at. And maybe tell me if I look happy or not to you?"

"I'm not sure it's as easy as all that," said Emba, remembering what Odolf had told her.

"Please," begged the man. "I'll give you the rest of my lunch... Two boiled eggs and another leg of chicken. You certainly seem to be enjoying that one by the sounds of it. Unless there's some kind of wild animal down there with you, making those loud chewing noises."

Boiled eggs and *chicken?* Emba could hardly believe her luck.

"And a big slab of fruit cake," he added, in case she needed any more convincing. But Emba was already scrambling to her feet. Already heading towards the pool.

The man dropped down out of the tree, sprinting past her towards the water's edge. "Wait while I stare into the depths for a few moments," he said, "and then tell me what you see."

"Mmhm," Emba agreed, sucking the last meaty scraps from her gnawed chicken leg. Her stomach was already gurgling with anticipation at the thought of another one.

"That's it," said the man. "Come and have a look now."

Emba stepped forwards, gazing into the dark, still waters of the pool. But there was nothing there.

"Erm, I don't think this is going to work," she said, "I can't see—" Wait, maybe there *was* something there… something moving beneath the surface of the water. Yes, she could make out proper colours and light now, shifting and rearranging themselves, taking shape. Emba stared down into the pool, transfixed by the slowly forming image before her. Except it wasn't an image of the man surrounded by his wife and children. It wasn't an image of the man at all…

"Oh!" She gasped out loud, reeling back in surprise as she realised what had happened. That must be *her* greatest fear she was looking at, not his. But it wasn't a life without Fred. It was nothing to do with Fred. And it wasn't Necromalcolm either. She didn't need to know what he looked like to realise that.

"What?" asked the man eagerly. "What did you see?"

But Emba was too shocked to answer. Her brain could barely form proper thoughts, let alone spoken words. *Dragon… Cave… But that looks like… no, no, no, that's impossible…*

She shut her eyes, hoping things might look different when she opened them again. No such luck. The ghostly dragon from the cave was still there, gazing back at her from under the water, its powerful wings stretched out against the dark reflected clouds. Even as Emba stood there, staring, the underwater clouds parted to reveal a big red crack in the sky behind it. But a mere crack was nothing compared to what else—*who* else—she could see in the pool. It was Emba herself, only she wasn't herself at all. Far from it.

The Emba in the pool didn't only have scales on her arms and legs, they were all over her body and face as well... and her tail. Yes, a tail! And as for her hands and feet—well, Fred's toenails looked positively normal by comparison. These were more like claws than nails. Sharp, gleaming dragon claws. It was her wings that were the most astonishing part of all though—beautiful boned wings, just like the dragon beside her. Emba felt a strange mixture of revulsion and longing as she tried to make sense of what she was seeing. Revulsion at the peculiar hybrid creature before her, and a deep yearning for the sky—for the cresting currents beneath her and the cooling rush of air against her face. Her stomach swooped and soared as she stood there, arms outstretched, fuelling the flickering fire in her chest.

"What are you doing?"

"Huh?" Emba pulled her arms back in, a hot blush spreading to her cheeks. For a moment there she'd forgotten all about the man. "I was just er…" *I was dreaming about what it would be like to fly.* "Just er… thinking. About… about your problem."

The man gazed at her expectantly. "And?"

"And it was hard to tell," she said. "I think sometimes our fears and longings are more closely interwoven than we realise."

"Did I look happy to you though? That's all I need to know."

"The thing is," Emba began, "I didn't actually…" But then she thought better of it. He might not give her any lunch if he knew the truth. "The thing is," she began again, "if you *really* want to know what your future holds, you'd be better off asking the Tome of

Terrible Tomorrows."

The man looked blank. "Never heard of it."

"It's an ancient book of prophecies," Emba explained. "My friend Fred, the Wise Hermit of Witchingford Wood, is the Tome's guardian." *And my guardian too. Oh Fred!* Emba swallowed down the lump in her throat and forced herself to keep going. "People come to her to discover the truth about their lives, and their futures," she told him, "and the Tome reveals the answers in a prophecy. They're a bit hard to decipher sometimes, but Fred always knows what they mean. I'm sure she'd be able to help you too."

"Witchingford Wood, you say? Perhaps I should pay this Fred of yours a visit." The man strode back towards his tree perch, reaching up into the branches to retrieve the rest of the lunch he'd promised her.

"Yes," said Emba. She wiped away a tear. "You really should. Only not just yet. She's not there at the moment—she's being held prisoner at Gravethorn Castle. That's where I'm headed now. I'm going to save her and bring her home."

The man pulled a face. "Rather you than me,"

he observed, handing over eggs and chicken and the biggest slice of fruit cake Emba had ever seen. "I've heard bad things about that place. They say the duchess is a fearsome woman. You don't want to get on the wrong side of her."

"I don't have any choice," said Emba. "If *I* don't save Fred, no one will." *Not even Odolf,* she thought bitterly.

"Well good luck to you then. And thank you for your help today..." The man broke off, squinting into the distance. "Speaking of the duchess, are those her soldiers I can see coming down the road now?"

It could have been soldiers, or horse thieves, or travelling monks. It could even have been a swarm of butterflies, given how bad his eyesight was. But Emba didn't stop to find out. The merest mention of soldiers was enough to send her body into high alert. To set her heart pounding in her chest again.

"Thank *you*," she replied, clutching the delicious-smelling food to her chest as she scooped up her bag and ran.

Chapter 15

The Shockingly Sharp Teeth of Terror

The panicked beating in Emba's chest took far longer to disappear than her lunch. She'd fully intended to save the fruitcake for later, having polished off the chicken and eggs as she cowered inside a hollow tree, hiding until she was certain the coast was clear. But somehow the fruitcake found its way into her mouth all the same and was soon nothing more than a delicious raisin-filled memory. Her other memories from her lunchtime stop were rather less agreeable though. The strange vision she'd seen in the water still haunted her as she began the long uphill trudge towards Gravethorn. What did it all mean? *I couldn't turn into a dragon if I tried. That's impossible. So how could that be my greatest fear? Mind you*, she thought,

I used to think dragons were impossible too, until I met one.

But if the pool hadn't reflected her greatest *fear*, it must have been her greatest desire instead. Which was clearly nonsense... wasn't it? For a moment, Emba imagined what it would be like, up there in the sky, with the world spread out beneath her. Imagined the beat of her wings and the powerful flick of her tail, with a beautiful bellyful of flames crackling inside her... *No, that's crazy,* she told herself, trying to ignore the answering heat in her stomach and throat. *That wasn't fire, that was...* Emba didn't know what it was, but surely fire would hurt more? *And what on earth would I want a tail for?* Wings might be handy though, she mused. Flying to the castle would be much quicker than walking.

Progress was certainly slow on this stretch of the journey. Emba was back amongst the trees again, following a narrow, snaking path through the oaks and beeches and shimmering gold fox firs that looked as if it might peter out at any moment. There were brambles too, with huge thorns that caught at her blanket as she passed, leaving a trail of torn threads in her wake. But Odolf had assured her that it was the shortest route to the castle—much quicker than sticking to the road. And he might well have been right, too, if she hadn't come to a fork in the path and gone the wrong way. If she hadn't realised too late that she was heading due east instead of north and tried to rectify her mistake by cutting across to the other path. If she hadn't found herself somewhere in the middle, with a deep growling sound coming from the undergrowth.

Raaggghhhrrrr.

A dragon? A boar?

A bear!

Stay calm, said a voice inside her head. *Don't panic*. But it was too late: Emba *was* panicking. She froze—apart from her legs, which were trembling like crazy—trying to remember what Fred had told her. Should she stand her ground and make a big noise? Try and frighten the creature away? Or should she play dead and hope for the best? But the voice inside her head was no help on that score. Her mind had gone blank. Blank of any *useful* information, anyway. All she could think of was the story Odolf had told them a few months before, about a cursed king who turned into a fierce bear every night, attacking his own beloved people. The curse could only be lifted by the moonlit kiss of a fearless maiden—yes, it was one of *those* stories— but in Odolf's version, the fearless maiden wasn't one for kissing. She stabbed the bear king through the heart with a butcher's knife after he savaged her pet dog, and was hung for treason the next day. It was a pretty gloomy story, really, and no help whatsoever when it came to Emba's current predicament.

If only I had a butcher's knife, she thought, the tremble in her legs spreading all the way up her body.

Raaggghhhrrrr.

No, Emba didn't have a knife, but she *did* have a scaring-off stone. She reached into her bag for it, as quietly and calmly as she could manage, and pulled out a half-eaten rotten turnip instead. *Hmm.* She couldn't remember *any* stories where the hero saved the day with half a turnip, but it was pleasingly heavy in her hand. *You could do a lot of damage with a well-aimed turnip to the head*, Emba thought to herself.

Hoped to herself.

Raaggghhhrrrrrrrrrr. The growling was getting louder each time. Louder and nearer. *Now what? Play dead? Hit it with the turnip? Or run?*

No, counselled the voice inside her head. *Whatever you do, don't run.*

But then the bear came charging through the trees in a blaze of brown fur and bared yellow teeth and Emba's legs decided for her. So much for the voice inside her head. She was running whether she liked it or not. Running and screaming.

"Helllpppppp!"

Grrrraaaahhhhh!

Emba pounded through the trees, zigzagging wildly as she ducked under low-hanging branches. The bear thundered after her, its mighty paws striking the ground with frightening force and speed.

Come on. Faster.

Agh! Watch out!

Emba scrambled over a rotten log, almost losing her footing in a tangled loop of ivy. It would take more than a bit of ivy to slow the bear though. It was gaining on her with every stumbling step now. With every ragged breath.

"Helllpppppp!

Grrraaahhhh roared the bear, louder and closer than ever.

Stop running, instructed a new voice in Emba's head. A voice which sounded oddly like Odolf. *And start fighting.*

Emba swung round with her turnip and took aim. The bear was only a few feet away. It was now or never.

Her arm whipped forward with lightning speed as she let go of the turnip, flinging it as hard and fast as she could.

Smack! It hit the bear on its snout, stopping it in its tracks.

Yes! Emba felt a tiny thrill of triumph as the bear reeled backwards in shock. It looked slightly less sure of itself now. Slightly less intent on ripping her open with its razor claws. But only slightly. It wasn't over yet...

Raaaahhhhrrr! came another roaring growl from behind her.

No, no, no! One bear had been bad enough, but *two?*

Start roaring, shouted the Odolf voice in her head. *And grab hold of that branch by your feet.* Only the voice wasn't coming from her head at all, Emba realised with a start of joy. It really *was* Odolf!

She spun around to see. Yes, there he was, pointing his wooden spear at the bear and looking every inch the brave warrior.

Emba picked up the branch and waved it in the air, roaring as if her life depended on it—which, in all honesty, it probably did. But if she *was* going to die in a bear attack, at least she wouldn't die alone now. And maybe, just maybe, the two of them together would be enough to make the bear back down.

Grrraaahhhh!

It wasn't giving up yet though. Half a turnip to the nose might have given the bear pause for thought but it hadn't knocked it out.

"That's it, keep roaring," shouted Odolf. "But don't make eye contact."

There wasn't much chance of that where Emba was concerned though. The bear's eyes were firmly trained on Odolf now, as if it was sizing him up. As if it was getting ready for another attack.

Emba felt a sudden spurt of anger, deep in her belly. Where moments before there'd been nothing but cold, quaking terror, now there was hot, rushing rage. Odolf had come back for her. He'd conquered his fears and stepped up when she needed him most. There was no way she was letting that bear hurt him.

"Don't even *think* about it," she roared, the words tearing out of her in a hot rush of smoke. "I don't care how big and scary you are, you stay away from my friend. Got it?"

"Emba!" cried Odolf. "Your mouth! You're... you're *smoking!* What's happening?"

But Emba didn't *know* what was happening. And she didn't have time to think about it, either. The fury inside of her was too hot for thoughts.

"I mean it," she roared at the bear through the swirling plumes of smoke. "Leave him alone!"

It was working! The bear let out a low moan, backing away as Emba bore down on it. And then, with a final bark of fright, it turned tail and ran.

Chapter 16

The Barbed Bottom Bite of Bravery

"Woah," said Odolf, staring at her in wide-eyed astonishment. At least, that's what he was doing when the smoke cleared enough for Emba to see. "What was *that?*"

"I don't know," Emba told him. The heat of her rage had cooled again now, leaving her sore-throated and worried, with a strange tingling sensation across her shoulders. "I've no idea." But that wasn't true. She was thinking of the vision she'd seen in the Pool of Perilous Perception. What if she really *was* turning into the strange human-dragon creature she'd seen reflected in the water? The idea didn't seem quite as impossible as it had before. When she reached inside the neck of her tunic to scratch her tingling shoulders, she could feel new scales pressing up through her skin.

"I thought that thing with your eyes was weird enough," said Odolf, "but *that* was something else."

Her eyes! Emba had forgotten about them. *Glowing.* That was the word he'd used, wasn't it? *And the black bits in the middle started flickering and changing shape.* Emba felt dizzy just thinking about it. First her eyes and now the smoke-breathing and extra scales... what was next? Wings...?

No. She shook the thought away again. This was exactly what Odolf had warned her about. He said people had been driven mad by the visions they'd seen reflected in the pool. Emba wasn't going to be one of them.

"Thank you for coming to my rescue," she said, changing the subject. "I didn't mean to run, I just panicked. And I certainly wasn't expecting *you* to turn up. I thought you'd be halfway home by now."

Odolf looked sheepish. "So did I," he said, his cheeks growing pink. "But the further I walked, the worse I felt. So I turned round and came back to find you, which would have been a lot easier if you'd stuck to the right path. It's a good job I spotted those bits of wool from your blanket, or I'd never have tracked you down. And then when I heard you screaming, I was worried I was too late."

"I'm so glad you changed your mind," said Emba. "I've never been more pleased to see anyone in my life."

Odolf's cheeks grew even pinker. "I might not be the big hero I always thought I was, but that doesn't mean I have to be a coward. And it was cowardly of me to leave you on your own like that. The thought of going back to the castle without my magic belt buckle still makes me feel sick with fear—I'll probably wet myself when the time comes—but the thought of losing Fred makes me feel even sicker. And the thought of losing you..." His cheeks were bright red now.

"Oh Odolf," cried Emba, throwing her arms round him. "That's the bravest thing I've ever heard you say."

"What? That I might wet myself when we reach the castle? That doesn't sound very heroic to me."

"There's more to bravery than bladder control," said Emba, wisely. "If you *weren't* scared about heading into untold danger, that would make you foolish, not brave. But to feel frightened and do it anyway… that's proper courage, that is. Forget about what it says in the Tome, *that's* what makes you a hero in *my* book."

Emba didn't need to see Odolf's face to know he was grinning. She could hear it in his voice. "But if the duchess *does* try to chop off my hands and head," he said, "can you do that thing with the smoke again? If it can scare off a wild bear, then maybe it'll work on her too."

Emba pulled away, her arms dropping back down to her sides. "I don't want to think about that," she said. "It's too…" She trailed away into silence, unable to say exactly *what* it was.

"Too weird?" Odolf guessed. "Too frightening? Too thrilling?"

"Too confusing," said Emba. Yes, it was definitely that. "Come on," she added. "We need to get back onto the proper path and get going. We've still got a long way to go before you wet yourself."

The rest of the long, wearisome journey passed without incident. Unless Odolf getting his foot stuck in a hagtail hole counted as an incident. Or Emba mistaking a rabbit dropping for a blackcurrant in the dark and almost throwing up on her own toes. But there were no more bears or fortune-telling ponds to deal with. No more dragon sightings or cracks in the sky. Just blisters and rumbling bellies and an unfortunate bite to the bottom, in Odolf's case, from a snapping witch fern. He scratched and grumbled as they plodded on into the night, too nervous to seek shelter again after the previous night's disaster. And when they couldn't walk any further, they curled up under the stars and Odolf scratched himself to sleep. He was still scratching when they finally emerged out of the trees the next morning to see the city of Gravethorn shimmering through the mist. There was a nervous edge to his scratching now though. It must have been the thought of returning to the scene of his crime. On the plus side, he hadn't wet himself yet.

"Wow, look at that," said Emba, gazing in wonder—and more than a little fear—at the sheer size of it. Her occasional trips to the town market with Fred had been overwhelming enough, but *this?* This was something else entirely. "We finally made it then. Which one's the castle?" she asked, taking in the big stone towers and imposing spires on the outskirts of the city.

"Are you serious?" asked Odolf, swapping hands and scratching some more. "It's that big, dark castle-shaped thing in the middle. You'd probably be able to see it better if you weren't standing behind a tree," he added helpfully.

Emba shuffled sideways, gasping out loud as the rest of the city revealed itself. It was vast. Vaster than vast. And there was the castle, towering over the giant sprawl of the city like a big black beetle. No, wait, not a beetle. It was more like a dragon, with spikes running along its back and a long, jagged wall wrapped tail-like round its body. Emba seemed to be seeing dragons *everywhere* lately.

"So now what?" she asked Odolf. "What's our next move?"

"*I* don't know," he said. "This was your idea."

No, thought Emba. *It was the Tome's, actually.* But it didn't really matter *whose* idea it was. Coming up with a foolproof rescue plan that didn't involve head-chopping or blood-draining was what mattered now. Which probably ruled out marching straight up to the castle and knocking on the door. That's what Necromalcolm would be expecting her to do, after all. It didn't seem like a particularly good way of avoiding the duchess either. No, they needed something altogether more cunning if they wanted to save Fred and get out of there alive.

"I thought things would seem a bit clearer once we actually got here," she admitted. "At least I *hoped* they would."

She replayed the rescue prophecy in her head, wondering if there were any clues she'd missed about the actual rescuing part:

Safety lies in walls of stone,
In promises to keep,
A stolen heart and broken art
Lies weeping in the deep.

Freedom calls the one who seeks
In tongues of pain and fire,
Bonds shall break and shackles shake
Before the hero's ire.

But if anything, it made even less sense than before. With Odolf's belt buckle gone, the only iron thing they had at their disposal was his helmet. And, despite what she might have told him in the barn, there was clearly nothing magic about *that*. It was basically just an oversized metal hat. How were they supposed to shake Fred's shackles and break her bonds now? Of course, the one person who *might* know the answer was Fred herself, which wasn't much help... unless... unless...

Yes, thought Emba. *That's it!* They didn't need to *rescue* her—at least, not yet. They only needed to *reach* her. And then Fred could tell them what to do. *She* could tell them what kind of 'ire' they needed to fulfil the prophecy and set her free.

"Did you ever see the dungeons when you worked at the castle?" she asked Odolf. "Would it be possible to get a message to one of the prisoners, do you think?"

Odolf shuddered. "Apart from the guards, the only people who got to see the dungeons were the prisoners themselves. And they didn't come back to tell us what they were like, funnily enough. If they did make it out again, it was only as far as the executioner's block..." His face had gone very pale all of a sudden. "I wish I still had my belt," he muttered.

"But there might be a way in you don't know about," said Emba, trying to stay hopeful. She didn't like the sound of that executioner's block either. Helping prisoners escape was probably pretty high up on the list of head-chopping-off offences. "Like a secret tunnel..." All the best castles had secret tunnels. At least, all the best castles in *stories* had secret tunnels.

Odolf thought for a moment, scratching his bitten bottom against the trunk of the tree to give his fingers a rest. "I remember my master saying *something* about an old tunnel system. It was built during the Great Siege of Gravethorn to smuggle food in through the enemy lines. But that was over a hundred years ago. It could have been filled in by now. And I've no idea where the entrance is, *or* whether it goes anywhere near the dungeons."

"I wonder if they were stone tunnels," said Emba. She was thinking of the prophecy again. "Safety lies in walls of stone… that's what the Tome said. Maybe it means we'll be safe as long as we keep to the tunnels." There were so many different ways of interpreting the same words; that was the problem.

"It's worth a try," agreed Odolf, "assuming we can find the way in. Mother Swails might be able to help us there."

"*Mother?*" Emba turned to him in surprise. "I thought you were an orphan."

"I am," said Odolf. "My parents died of the Sweating Plague after I started my apprenticeship with the blacksmith... Mum first, and then Dad. And then all three of my sisters…" He fell quiet for a moment, lost in his own memories.

Emba reached over and squeezed his hand. Fred had been all the mother she'd ever needed, and the mere thought of losing her was like a knife through the heart. Was that what it was like for Odolf? Is that why he never talked about his family? Because the pain was still too fierce?

Odolf blinked away a tear and sniffed loudly. And then he shook his head, as if he was shaking himself back to the present. "Mother Swails isn't *my* mother," he explained. "That's just what everyone calls her. She's the barmaid at the tavern on Hangman's Lane, which means she gets to hear *all* the castle gossip. If anyone knows anything about those tunnels it's her."

Emba wasn't sure she liked the sound of Hangman's Lane very much, but a visit to Mother Swails sounded like their best plan. Their only plan. "Alright," she agreed. "Let's see what she has to say. Maybe she'll be able to tell us more about Fred too—about which bit of the dungeons they're keeping her in. And maybe some more information about Necromalcolm," she added with a shiver. "That would be useful as well." Had he already set up camp at the castle, with his blood-collecting barrel? Did he have henchmen posted along the ramparts, watching out for their arrival?

She glanced up into the sky, half-expecting to see the red crack again. To feel the rush of invisible wings overhead, beating out a fresh warning: *Beware,*

beware, beware. But there was no crack today, just a soft, clouded mist. And the only beating she could hear was her own heart. Maybe that was a good sign, Emba told herself. Maybe she didn't *need* warning today. Maybe her luck really *had* changed this time.

Chapter 17

The Shockingly Short Spell of Fortune

Odolf led the way, checking over his shoulder every five seconds and jumping at the slightest sound. And there were a *lot* of sounds to jump at once they were inside the city gates: squawking chickens, screaming babies, clattering carts, clopping hooves, the cries of market men selling their wares, the warning cries of women emptying chamber pots out of windows into the street below... Noises and smells (and the contents of chamber pots) flew at them from every direction.

If anything, Emba felt safer *inside* the city than out though. She felt less visible amongst the jostling crowds. Less conspicuous. Even if Necromalcolm and his henchmen were keeping watch for her arrival, they'd struggle to pick her out from the general throng.

She was more worried about getting separated from Odolf, knowing she'd be well and truly lost without him. Every winding street looked the same as all the others to her. But at last they turned into an open square with a huge wooden scaffold at its centre. *The hangman's gallows*, thought Emba. *We must be nearly there.*

She was right. Odolf checked over his shoulder one last time, and then turned sharply to the right, ducking in through the back door of a large, ramshackle building. Emba ducked in after him.

"Welcome to The Hangman's Arms," said Odolf under his breath. He took off his helmet and tucked it under his arm. "The roughest tavern in the whole of Gravethorn. Try not to let anyone see your scales—we don't want to attract any unwanted attention to ourselves—and keep close to me."

Emba nodded, remembering how the man with the cart had reacted the day before. Now wasn't the time to remind Odolf that she was just the same as everyone else on the inside, no matter what she looked like on the outside. Besides, she wasn't even sure it was true anymore. She wrapped her blanket round her like a shawl and followed him (and the overpowering smell of beer) into the heat and noise of the tavern.

"What can I do for you, my lovelies?" asked a round-faced lady with a thick mop of curly hair and red, sweating cheeks. Was that Mother Swails? She beamed at them both, over her tray of tankards. "Nice bit of pie?"

Pie, growled Emba's stomach. *Mmm yes please.*

Odolf licked his lips. "That sounds so good," he murmured. "*So* good. I haven't eaten properly in days... but no, no thank you," he added, blinking hard, as if it hurt him physically to turn it down. "We don't have any money for food. We just wanted to ask you a few questions."

Mother Swails reached over and pinched his cheek. "You poor wee thing. You're wasting away there. Tell you what. How about I rustle up some burnt pastry scraps and a spot of yesterday's lamb stew for you both?" she added. "I usually feed the leftovers to the dogs, but I reckon you could use it more. And then I'll see if I can help you with your questions."

Odolf nodded furiously. He seemed to have lost the power of speech all of a sudden.

"Oh, yes please," said Emba, answering for the both of them. "That would be lovely."

And it was. Burnt pastry and cold congealed lamb stew had never tasted so good. Emba would have licked the bowl out afterwards if she could, but she was still trying to keep a low profile.

"Now then," said Mother Swails. "What was it you wanted to ask me?"

Odolf cleared his throat. "We were wondering if you knew anything about the—"

But he never got to finish the question.

"That's him," came a furious cry from behind. "That's the filthy little thief who stole the duchess's belt buckle."

Chapter 18

The Castle of Calamitous Fate

A huge bear of a man with a thick, wiry beard and a crooked nose came barging across the room towards them, elbowing people out of the way in his fury. "I'd recognise that thieving, one-eyebrowed little face anywhere," he growled, pointing at their table.

"M-m-master!" stammered Odolf, looking like he might be about to bring his burnt pastry and cold stew back up again. "W-what are you doing here?"

"What am *I* doing here, you snivelling, ungrateful wretch? I'm on a well-earned ale break after an early start at the forge today. Do you remember the forge? The one I left you in charge of? The one you stole this helmet from?" He scooped the helmet up off the table as he said it, putting it on his own head for safekeeping. "And the duchess's belt buckle?"

Odolf gulped. "Y-yes, of course I remember. I didn't *mean* to steal them though. I'm sorry. I just panicked."

But the blacksmith hadn't finished yet. "Do you know how much trouble you left behind when you ran off with that buckle? When you left *me* to deal with the duchess? I was lucky to keep my job. I was lucky to keep my *head*. If it hadn't been for my quick talking and my solemn vow to stick *your* miserable head on a spike myself when the soldiers caught you, I'd have been for the chop."

"I'm sorry," said Odolf again. "I never meant for you to get into trouble. I never meant for any of it."

"And I don't suppose you *meant* to come snivelling back again like a miserable thieving worm either," said the blacksmith, wiping his nose with a hairy knuckle. "And yet here you are. What *are* you doing here? That's the real question, isn't it? And which way shall I put your head on the spike? Forwards or backwards? That's *two* questions, in fact."

"N-neither?" suggested Odolf. "How about we just pretend this never happened? That you never saw me? The last thing we want to do is upset the duchess again…"

"Upset her?" said the blacksmith. "Nonsense. She'll be thrilled to have it back. That belt buckle was one of a kind. Irreplaceable. Magic like that only works once, doesn't it?"

Odolf glanced sideways at Emba, as if to say, *see, I* told *you it was magic*. Or maybe it was more of a *help-I don't-want-to-have-my-head-on-a-spike-forwards*-or-*backwards* kind of glance. Emba couldn't quite decide.

"But Odolf doesn't *have* the belt buckle anymore," she said. "If anyone needs their head putting on a spike it's that horse thief. The one who thought I was a snake. *He's* the one you should be looking for."

The blacksmith turned to stare at her, as if he'd only just noticed she was there. "What horse thief? Why would he think you were a snake?"

Emba held out her arm to show him, ignoring what Odolf had said earlier. The time for keeping a low profile had well and truly passed. Every eye in the tavern was fixed on them now.

"Sssssss," she hissed, in the vain hope that the blacksmith might be scared off as easily as the thief had been.

But she was out of luck. "Hmm, a thief *and* a freak," he said, looking decidedly *un*scared. "Maybe I'll throw you in as a bonus... I heard she's looking for a new fool."

"Throw me in where?" Emba wasn't sure she understood. "Who's he calling a fool?"

"He means he's going to hand *you* over to the duchess as well," whispered Odolf. "Quick, do your smoke thing again, it's our only chance. Blind him with the smoke and then make a run for it."

It was a good idea. No, it was a *great* idea. Only Emba didn't have the first clue how to go about it.

She shut her eyes and screwed up her nose, thinking hot, smoky thoughts.

Come on... start wisping. Start swirling.

She squeezed her hands into fists and puffed out her cheeks, trying to force a fresh plume out of her mouth.

"Are you alright, my love?" she heard Mother Swails asking. "Touch of constipation, is it?"

Come on. You can do it. Start smoking.

But it was no good. All Emba managed to squeeze out was a lamb-flavoured burp. Where was the fiery feeling in her belly when she needed it? The only thing in her stomach now was a cold knot of worry. What would the duchess do to them? What if Necromalcolm was there too? And what about Fred? How were they supposed to save her now?

"Come on," said the blacksmith. "On your feet, the pair of you. My morning ale will have to wait. It's payback time."

I was right about my luck changing, thought Emba, as the blacksmith hauled them through the city, dragging them along by the scruffs of their necks. *Only it changed for the worse.*

"Please," she begged as they arrived, panting, at the top of a steep flight of steps. The dark stone walls of the castle towered above them. "Please don't do this. We don't want to cause any trouble. We're just here to help a friend." Officially speaking, breaking a prisoner out of the dungeons probably *did* count as trouble, but now wasn't the time to be splitting hairs. Now was the time for pleading and praying and panicking. No, not panicking. Panicking wouldn't get them anywhere. What Emba needed now was a plan. She was out of luck on that score too though.

The blacksmith took no notice, marching them straight over the drawbridge towards the spiked metal teeth of the portcullis.

"Halt!" roared the sentry guards, barring the way with their sharp-ended pikes. "Who goes there?"

"Roger Weldon, the blacksmith," came the reply. "With prisoners for the duchess. Tell her I've caught the light-fingered little rat who stole her brother's belt buckle, and his strange snaky friend."

"No," said Emba, thinking fast. Maybe she *did* have a plan, after all. "Tell her Emba Oak is here to see Necromalcolm. And if he wants my blood, he'll have to let Odolf and Fred go."

It might not have been the *best* plan she'd ever had. In fact, as plans went, handing yourself over to the enemy was pretty much a last option. But if it meant saving Fred and Odolf, it had to be worth a shot. One prisoner was better than three. She was the one who'd got them into this mess—it was only fair that she got them out again.

Besides, maybe this Necromalcolm wasn't as evil as everyone made out. Maybe he wouldn't take *all* of her blood. Maybe he'd settle for a little pinprick. A scratch.

"What are you doing?" asked Odolf. "Are you crazy?"

"What's she on about?" asked the guards. "Is she mad?"

"Take me to Necromalcolm," Emba demanded, a little louder than before. "And let the others go."

The guards looked blank. "Who's Necromalcolm?"

"Search me," said the blacksmith, with a shrug.

What? This wasn't the way Emba's last-resort plan was supposed to go.

"Nec-ro-mal-colm," she said again, super slowly and clearly.

"Never heard of him," said the first guard.

"Or her," added the second guard helpfully. "Could be a lady."

"Necromalcolm," Emba said again, her voice

turning oddly squeaky as she tried not to cry. They *must* have heard of him. This *had* to be the right place. Otherwise…

The first guard was laughing now. "Sounds like a mouse's name when you say it like that."

Emba blinked back her tears, put on her lowest, deepest voice and tried one last time: "NECROMALCOLM."

"No," chuckled the second guard. "That's too deep for a mouse. More like a cow, I'd say."

Emba really *was* starting to panic now. Panic with a side hint of despair. As last-resort plans went, this one was *not* going according to plan at all. "But you must know who he is. He kidnapped our friend, Fred…"

Three blank faces (and one scared Odolf face) stared back at her.

"…The Wise Hermit of Witchingford Wood."

Still no reaction.

"And he left a note saying to come here if I wanted to save her…"

Still nothing. Maybe his fame didn't extend beyond the magic community.

"…from a calamitous fate," finished Emba, hopelessly.

"What does 'calamitous' mean?" asked the first guard.

The others shrugged. "Dunno," said the second. "But it doesn't sound good, does it?"

Emba pulled the bedraggled note out of her bag to show them. "I *thought* it was telling us to come here," she said, her despair deepening with every passing moment. "But the ink was all smudged and we couldn't make out the last word." The entire *letter* was one big smudge now, after two days jostled up in her wet bag. "But we asked the Tome of Terrible Tomorrows and *it* said for us to come here and… and…" *And nothing.* The Tome hadn't actually mentioned Gravethorn by name, had it? But maybe Necromalcolm hadn't arrived yet, she told herself. Or maybe he was here undercover. Maybe *that's* why nobody had heard of him. Yes, that *had* to be it, otherwise… And there it was again, that miserable lurking 'otherwise'. *Otherwise this entire trip has been for nothing… Otherwise we've wasted all this time and we* still *don't know where Fred is…*

"Just give the duchess my message anyway," she told the guards. "Don't worry about the Necromalcolm bit. Tell her Emba Oak, the girl with dragon skin, is here to save the Wise Hermit of Witchingford Wood. She'll know what it means."

"We won't be telling the duchess anything," said the first guard. "She's gone."

What? Every time Emba thought her heart couldn't sink any lower, it managed to prove her wrong.

Odolf seemed rather more cheered by the news though. "She's gone? As in moved away? Well we might as well go then too."

"No, gone as in gone out to choose a new executioner's block," said the first guard. "That last one we had only lasted fifty head-choppings. The duchess has had men scouring every inch of woodland in the dukedom, looking for the perfect specimen, and now she's gone to pick her favourite."

"Yeah," agreed the second guard. "And the only place *you'll* be going in the meantime is the dungeons."

The dungeons? At least we'll know for sure if Fred's here or not, thought Emba, clinging to what little silver lining her darkening clouds had left. *And if she's not? I guess we're officially doomed.*

Chapter 19

The Dungeons of Desperate Doom

Their doom was official now. Emba and Odolf had been down in the dark, dank dungeons for what felt like hours, and there was still no sign of Fred. No matter how hard they shouted and called, there was no answering cry from their friend. Emba thought she heard a hoarse whispery voice rasping back from one of the other cells—"Keep the noise down will you? Some of us are trying to die down here..."—but it definitely wasn't Fred.

There wasn't much they could do to look for her, other than calling though. It was too dark to see anything, and the heavy chains holding them to the wall didn't allow for further exploration of their prison quarters. So once they'd finished shouting and calling—and taking turns to blame each other for their pitiful plight—there was nothing left to do but wait. And weep. And wish they'd never come.

Emba sank back against the cold slime of the wall and shut her eyes in defeat. Maybe the hoarse-voiced prisoner had the right idea. If they *were* going to die down here, they might as well get on with it. It was either that or wait for the duchess to get back and chop off their heads. But she must have been dreaming instead of dying, because the dungeon seemed to grow lighter, even as she sat there. The air felt different too—clearer and brighter, somehow. Fresher. Yes, that was it—fresher. And what was that noise she could hear? A soft rhythmic pulsing... a beating... a beating of wings...

Emba didn't need to open her eyes to know the dragon was back. But she opened them all the same— in her dream she opened them, anyway—and there it was, shimmering above her, the glow of its silvery wings lighting up the dungeon like a beacon of hope. Of escape. Emba longed to fly away with it. To feel the rush of air against her scaled skin. To shake off her misery and failure and leave it all behind. But the dragon wasn't calling for her to join it. Not this time. It wanted to show her something. A different kind of escape.

Emba watched in wonder as the dragon flew down, like a huge silvery bird, landing beside her with a soft, velvet thud. She should have been scared as it leaned in towards her with a single knife-like claw extended, but she wasn't. Even in the dream she knew it wouldn't hurt her. And she was right. It was reaching for the heavy padlock on her shackles. It was threading its claw into the hole and turning it like a key. And it was working! The padlock sprang open with a satisfying click and Emba's wrists were free.

"Thank you," she said, stretching up to touch the creature's gleaming snout. "Thank you for saving me." But something jerked her back again, pulling her back to the wall with a painful jolt. *Smack* went her head against the slimy stone.

"What are you doing?" Odolf hissed. "Who are you talking to?"

What? Emba blinked in the darkness. *Where was*

the dragon?

"I er…" Disappointment flooded through her veins. "It must have been a dream," she said, staring down at her still-shackled wrists. Not that she could see them anymore—the light had vanished along with the dragon. But she could feel them alright. Could feel the cold weight of metal against the invisible line where her scales met her skin. Emba closed her eyes again in case the dream was still there, waiting for her. But there was nothing to see anymore. Nothing but the inky black underside of her own eyelids. *If only I had dragon claws instead of scales*, she thought. *I could pick the lock myself then…*

"Wait, that's it!" she cried. "Toenails!"

"Toenails?" asked Odolf. "I think you might *still* be dreaming."

"No, I'm awake. And I've got a plan. A plan to get us out of here," Emba added, in case he was expecting something more foot-related. "But I'll need your help. I don't think I can get the angle right with these shackles on." She shuffled along the floor towards him. "I'm going to hold up my leather pouch and I need you to reach across and get one of Fred's toenail shards out for me."

"Ew. Do I have to?" said Odolf.

"Don't think of it as a bit of toenail," said Emba. "Think of it as a key. A gnarly, yellow-brown key. Please, just give it a try."

"I'll do my best."

Emba wriggled as ticklish fingers brushed the end of her nose. "Oi, get off, that's my face," she said. "Down a bit... No, that's my neck. Down a bit further."

"Found it!" Odolf declared at last. "At least I *think* I have." He fell quiet for a moment. Emba could hear him breathing hard with concentration. Could feel the pull on her pouch as he worked his fingers inside. "There! I've got one. Now what? Wait a minute," he went on before Emba could answer. "Are you sure this is a good idea? What if the shards have to stay inside the leather pouch to stop Necromalcolm from seeing you in his scrying bowl?"

"I don't think it matters anymore," said Emba. "He already found me. Besides, we're the ones looking for him now." *Or at least we will be, once we get out of here.* "Now you need to find the lock on my shackles and open it with the toenail."

"Will it be strong enough?" Emba could hear the doubt in Odolf's voice.

"Yes, of course it will," she said firmly, trusting in her dream. Trusting in the gnarly, naily power of her guardian's hard-grown gift. "You heard what Fred said—it took her twenty-seven years to grow it and a full day and a half to saw through it. It must be pretty strong."

"Or she didn't have a very good saw," observed Odolf. But he did as he was asked, feeling round Emba's wrists with his spare hand, patting and stroking her like a dog. "I think I've got it," he said. "Yes, that feels like a lock. I still don't think this is going to work, but..."

Click!

Emba didn't just hear the click, she felt it too. She felt the spring of release round her wrists and the giddy rush of freedom.

"We did it!" she cried. "*You* did it, I mean. Here, pass me the toenail shard so I can do yours and then we'll do the same with our ankle locks. And then when the guard comes for us, we'll knock him out with a heavy bit of chain and make our escape." Emba was thinking of the skinny-legged prison guard who'd brought them down to the dungeons and shackled them to the wall. Provided they planned their ambush properly, the two of them should be able to overpower him. Hopefully he wouldn't know what was coming until it was too late.

"Alright," agreed Odolf, reaching for Emba's hand and pressing the toenail shard into her waiting palm. "What have we got to lose? Apart from our heads, I mean."

"Nothing," said Emba. "If Fred is down here somewhere, we'll find her. And if not, the sooner we get away from here the better."

It was a good plan. No, it was better than good. It was a *great* plan. And it was working too. Emba fished a second shard out of her pouch for Odolf, once his hands were free, so they could double their efforts. Two toenail keys were quicker than one. Not quick enough though...

Emba was so dazzled by the sudden burst of light when the door opened, she forgot all about clunking anyone over the head with a bit of chain. She was too busy shrinking back into the shadows and shielding her eyes from the glare. Not that they'd have been able to do much escaping anyway, with Odolf's ankles still clamped in irons. His ankle lock must have been stiffer than hers. And it wasn't the skinny-legged guard who'd come for them this time either. It was four big burly guards with blazing torches—and sharp-looking swords—versus one-and-a-half free prisoners with their hands clamped over their eyes. It was hardly a fair match.

"You," said the biggest and burliest of the guards, waving his sword in their direction. "The duchess wants to see you."

"Me?" asked Odolf. "I d-didn't mean to steal it—her brother's b-belt buckle, I mean. And it was a long time ago now. I'm not sure her brother would have liked it anyway," he gabbled. "It wasn't even that magic. It couldn't have been because I tripped over a rock when I was wearing it once, and really hurt my knee—"

"No, *her*," interrupted the guard. "The girl with the scales. The duchess didn't mention anything about weedy boys with missing eyebrows. But if you're the one who took that buckle, you'd better come along too. I imagine she'll have a few questions for you as well. And by questions, I mean horrible painful punishments." He pulled a key out of his pocket and released Odolf from his ankle shackles. "And *I'll* have some questions for Derek, when I see him, about why you're not chained up properly."

Odolf gulped. "Me and my stupid big mouth," he mumbled. "I should have kept quiet."

But Emba was too busy puzzling over the guard's words to offer any comfort. Not the bit about Derek (whoever he was), but the bit about the duchess asking for the girl with the scales. Why would the duchess be interested in *her?* Did that mean Necromalcolm *was* at the castle after all? But then where was Fred? Why hadn't she answered any of their calls and shouts? And where did the duchess's brother fit into it all?

Emba didn't have long to puzzle though. Rough hands hauled her to her feet and marched her up the spiral stone staircase with Odolf following behind, whimpering softly under his breath.

"Ah, there you are, Derek," said the head guard as they emerged back into the main body of the castle and came face-to-face with the skinny-legged guard from before. "I thought I told you to chain them up good and proper," he snarled. "So how come the girl was wandering round free as a bird? It won't do, Derek, d'you hear me? I've a good mind to report you to the duchess for dereliction of duty…"

Emba didn't know what 'dereliction of duty' meant but it seemed pretty serious, judging by the terrified look on Derek's face. "It's not Derek's fault," she piped up. "It's… it's…" She was about to explain about Fred's toenails, but then had a better idea. "It's because of the prophecy, you see… in the Tome of Terrible Tomorrows… It says that the er… the chosen ones—that's us—can't be tamed by mortal chains. And anyone who crosses us will meet a terrible end. A *calamitous* end, in fact. So if Fred *is* here, I suggest you hand her over, this instant, and let us go, before anyone gets hurt." How was *that* for a spot of quick thinking? Would it be enough to convince him though?

No. It wouldn't.

"Nice try," said the head guard. "I don't know who this Fred character is, but I *do* know that the duchess'll have my head on the block if I let you go. Come on, hurry up now," he told the other guards. "We don't want to keep her waiting."

Emba and Odolf were marched across the central courtyard and up another winding staircase, into an impressive room lined with rich red and gold tapestries. And there, sitting on her bejewelled silver throne, was the duchess. At least, Emba assumed that's who she was.

"Here we are, Your Grace," said the guard, thrusting Emba down onto her knees in front of the throne. "Here's the prisoner you asked for."

"And here's one you *didn't* ask for," said another of the guards, pushing Odolf down beside her. "The little thief who stole—and lost—your brother's belt buckle. Good job you got that new executioner's block, Your Grace," he added. "I'll go and get it ready, shall I?"

Chapter 20

The Not-so-Little Brother of Badness

The duchess was a tall, thin-faced woman with high cheekbones and dark, glittering eyes. They weren't glittering in a nice way though, Emba thought to herself. They weren't glittering with kindness, or joy, or merriment over a funny joke about donkeys. It was more like malice.

"So," drawled the duchess, beckoning Emba forwards with a long, curled finger. "*You're* the girl my little brother's been searching for all these years, are you?"

What? Emba gaped at her in confusion. First Necromalcolm, and now the duchess's brother? Why was *he* looking for her?

The duchess cupped her hand under Emba's chin

and tilted her face up to the light. "You've certainly got the yellow eyes. And the scaled skin, of course." She laughed a mean, humourless laugh. "How funny. All these years he's spent, scouring the globe for this so-called dragon-blooded child, and then you turn up at *my* castle. And with his buckle-stealing thief to boot."

She turned her dark, glittering gaze on Odolf. "Yes, the belt-buckle thief," she said, softly. "A rather *careless* thief, by all accounts, if you've lost it already. Foolish, and brazen too, returning to the scene of the crime. Did you honestly think I'd have forgotten what you did? Did you think I'd have *forgiven* you?"

Odolf was shaking violently. "N-no, Your G-Grace. I didn't think that. I thought you'd probably ch-chop off my hands… or my head… but I came anyway. To help my friend. I am sorry though, Your Grace. I never meant to take it. And I never meant to *lose* it either."

Emba reached out for his trembling hand and held it, tight.

"Hmm," said the duchess thoughtfully. "There's nothing I'd like more than to chop off your hands and head and string you up by your feet, but it was Malc's belt buckle. Or at least it would have been if you hadn't stolen it. It's only fair that *he* should be the one to choose your punishment. Don't worry though, I'm sure it will be fiendishly clever and horrid, whatever he decides. Malc really is quite brilliant when it comes to magic. Apart from that one fateful spell of course," she added, glaring at Emba.

"*Malc*, did you say?" asked Emba, struck by a sudden thought. "That's not short for Necro*malc*olm, by any chance, is it?"

"It's short for *Malcolm*," the duchess snarled. "He added the Necro bit after he took up dark magic and necromancy—all that summoning spirits out of their graves to do his bidding stuff. But he'll always be plain old Malc to me."

Emba's insides lurched with a mixture of excitement and fear. "And is he here? The guards didn't know who I was talking about but maybe I should have asked for Malc, instead. And Fred? What about her?"

The duchess glared at her. "Of course he's not here," she snapped. "You of all people should know that."

"What do you mean? Why should *I* know that?" *And what about Fred? You still haven't answered my question.*

But the duchess took no notice. She seemed lost in her own thoughts. "Maybe now he'll finally get to put that right." She clicked her fingers at the guards. "Take them to my brother at the Grey Tower," she said.

The Grey Tower? thought Emba. *Was* that *where Necromalcolm's note had told them to go? Was that where he was keeping Fred?*

"And make sure they're properly bound and shackled. *Especially* the girl. We can't risk losing her again. In fact, take the prison cart to be on the safe side. I'll send a hawk on ahead and tell him to expect you." The duchess smiled to herself. "I almost wish I was coming too—I'd love to see the look on little Malc's face when he finally gets to meet her. But I promised the executioner I'd watch tomorrow's beheadings—you know how it is," she added, turning back to Odolf.

"Y-y-yes, Your Grace. I remember."

Emba shivered. Chopping off hands and heads didn't sound like the sort of thing you'd forget very easily. No wonder Odolf had been scared to come back. Whatever punishment Necromalcolm came up with, surely it couldn't be as bad as his sister's. Could it?

"Well don't just stand there then," the duchess roared at the guards. "Take them away."

"Excuse me," said Emba, calling through the cage bars as the prison cart rumbled on into the gathering darkness. Her ankles and wrists were back in shackles again, and there was an extra chain round her waist, fixing her to the cage wall. It would take more than a toenail shard to get out of *this*, even if she wanted to… which she didn't… not really. Because no matter how terrifying the thought of meeting Necromalcolm was, at least she was finally on her way to Fred. *No more false starts this time*, she told herself. *No more stupid mistakes.* "Excuse me," she called again.

"Nope. You heard what I said," grunted the nearest

guard. "No more toilet breaks." They'd barely left Gravethorn when Odolf's nerves—and bladder—had got the better of him. And after the third stop in a row, the guard had clearly had enough.

"No, it's not that," said Emba. "I just wanted to ask about this Malc fellow. The duchess's brother, I mean. Do you ever see him at the castle? What's he like?"

The guard shook his head. "Of course I haven't seen him at the castle. He never leaves the tower, does he?" He dropped his voice to a low whisper. "And the duchess doesn't like visiting him, either. That's what they say, anyway. It makes her too upset. All that stuff about needing to be there for the executions tomorrow... I think that was just an excuse."

"But *why* doesn't he leave the tower?" asked Emba. It didn't make any sense. Didn't the duchess say that he'd been searching the globe for her?

"Enough with the stupid questions," snapped the guard. "We've got a long journey ahead of us tonight. Why don't you take a leaf out of your friend's book and get some sleep? Although preferably *without* the pig-like snoring."

Sleep? thought Emba, listening to the rhythmic snorts and rumbles coming from Odolf's side of the cage. How was she expected to sleep with an empty stomach and a head full of thoughts and questions battling for her attention? *Is Necromalcolm some kind of recluse, who refuses to leave his own tower? Is that why he needs his scrying bowl? But why would that upset the duchess when she sees him? Maybe he's given up washing himself too,* Emba thought. *Maybe he's let his beard grow really long and scruffy, with wild animals nesting inside it… Not just lice, but moths and beetles and mice… Oh no, what if he's got snakes nesting in there too?*

No. Emba didn't want to think about snakes. She leaned back against the bars and shut her eyes, trying to think of something nice instead. She imagined she was back in her nice warm bed in the cave, with a belly full of warm goat's milk, and Fred sat beside her, the old woman's chin whiskers glinting in the candlelight. She imagined Fred's gnarly hands tucking her in under her blanket, just like when she was little, and singing her to sleep:

"Keep me safe in sleep tonight
From murderous tooth and claw,
From flashing blade and bloodied sword
And monsters bathed in gore."

But the words seemed to shift and change as the steady rumble of the cart rocked Emba from side to side. From side to side to side…

"Keep me safe from unwashed harm,
From trailing beards and snakes,
From lice, and bugs and mouldy crumbs
Of bread and meat and cakes.
Keep my blood within my veins
And make me brave and true,
Guide me on my way to Fred
And show me what to do…"

And then her dream dragon was back, flying Emba through the darkening sky towards a tall, gleaming tower of grey skulls. And there was Necromalcolm—watching from the very top—with his long, unwashed hair and even longer beard of snakes streaming out like ribbons.

"You! Egg Girl," roared Dream Necromalcolm as

Emba flew nearer. "Give me your blood—*all* your blood—or the old lady DIES!"

"No," screamed Emba as she realised Fred was there with him. As she saw Necromalcolm swing her upside down and dangle her over the side of the tower by her toenails. "Nooooooo!"

And then Odolf was nudging her awake with his foot, telling her that it was only a dream. Telling her everything was going to be alright. Telling her to stop wailing before the guard had her gagged. "He said my snoring was bad enough, but he drew the line at screaming..."

Emba looked round in confusion, blinking in the darkness. The tower was gone, along with Fred. Along with Necromalcolm and his beard of snakes. Instead, she found herself back in the prison cart with Odolf, bumping along under a cold, star-studded sky. But the fear stayed with her, long after the dream had faded into memory, growing and swelling as the full enormity of the task ahead sank in. And the closer they got to Necromalcolm, the bigger that task seemed. *Finding Fred was only the first part of the challenge*, she told herself, miserably, *and you did a pretty poor job of that, all things considered. What makes you think you'll be any better at* saving *her? Not to mention saving yourself, and Odolf...*

The cart rumbled on into the night, as the last of Emba's hope and bravery slunk away through the bars of her cage. All the challenges she'd faced so far—the magpike and the thieves, the bear attack, imprisonment in the castle dungeons—were nothing, she realised, compared to what lay ahead.

Chapter 21

The Only (Awful) Way is Up

Necromalcolm's tower was nothing like the tower in Emba's dream. It didn't gleam in the early morning light, and it wasn't made of skulls. It *was* tall though. Ridiculously tall. Emba felt dizzy just looking at it, disappearing off into the soft wisps of cloud overhead. *So that's where he lives*, she thought, shivering as the guards unlocked the shackles round their ankles and helped them down out of the cart. She'd finally found him then—the wicked necromancer who'd been searching for *her* all these years. Who'd stolen away the only mother she'd ever known and was waiting, somewhere inside, to drain her blood.

Her legs were stiff after so long chained up in the cage, and her neck ached where she'd fallen asleep at an awkward angle. But Emba craned her head back all the same, tilting her face towards the top of the tower. Towards the big red crack opening up behind the smoke-like wisps of cloud, even as she stood there, watching. It looked like a bleeding wound stretching across the sky. This was the end—she could feel it. The end of her journey. The end of her story. But what if it was the end of *her* as well?

She was still staring up into the sky when an identical-looking pair of huge, leather-clad henchmen emerged from the bottom of the tower to meet them. Everything about them seemed the same, from their thick, low-lying eyebrows to their crooked teeth and matching dark bushy beards. They even spoke the same, talking in perfect unison:

"Our master thanks you. We'll take them from here," they told the duchess's guards. One took hold of the chain round Emba's waist, and started marching her towards the tower door, while the other took hold of Odolf's and followed along behind.

"That's him," hissed Odolf, loud enough for everyone to hear. "That's the beardy man I was telling you about. The man who was asking questions about you in the woods the other week. No, wait, maybe it was the other one. Do you think they're twins?"

"Twins?" spat Emba's henchman before she could answer. "*Twins?* We're nothing of the sort. *I'm* the original me and he's my doppelgänger—my double. One of three other doubles, in fact. *That's* how clever the master is. It's hard work looking after him, with so many stairs to climb, so he conjured up a whole team of other me's to help out."

Emba didn't know much about dark magic—nothing at all, in fact—but conjuring up people out of thin air sounded pretty dark indeed. Dark and powerful. An icy shiver snaked its way down her back as they approached the carved dragon-mouth doorway, with its sharpened rows of teeth. What chance would she have against someone with that kind of power? It made Fred's toenail charm seem like child's play.

"Don't listen to him," replied Odolf's beardy henchman, his top lip curling upwards in a sneer. "*I'm* the original."

"No, you're not," snorted Emba's. "I was here for

years before you came along."

"You mean *I* was…"

"It doesn't matter which one of you is the original," said Emba, thinking quickly. They were inside the tower now, at the bottom of a dizzying series of interwoven staircases, twisting up and away in every direction. Which one would lead them to Fred? "All *we're* interested in is who can tell us where the Wise Hermit of Witchingford Wood is. The old lady with the silver hair and long toenails. Is your master keeping her here, at the tower? Is she safe?" *Please let her be safe. Please don't let me be too late.*

"Oh yes," the henchmen answered in unison. "The old woman's down in the cellar."

The cellar! Of course that's where she'd be, thought Emba, remembering the prophecy:

A stolen heart and broken art

Lies weeping in the deep.

But there were no stairs leading down, just a big round metal cover in the centre of the dragon mosaic floor. *Oh Fred!* Was she under there now, chained up and weeping as in the prophecy? The thought was like a physical pain in Emba's chest—a searing heat, burning into her heart. If it wasn't for her own shackles and chain, she'd have ripped the cover off there and then with her bare hands. Tried to, anyway.

"And nothing *calamitous* has happened to her yet?" she asked, fighting back hot salty tears.

The henchmen shrugged. "That depends. What does 'calamitous' mean?"

"I don't know," Emba admitted. "That's the problem. And what about 'ire'? I don't suppose you know what *that* means, do you? *Is* it short for 'iron'?"

She was thinking of the last lines in the prophecy now:

Bonds shall break and shackles shake
Before the hero's ire.

But time was running out. If they didn't solve the riddle soon, and get to the heroic rescuing part, it might be too late. Too late to save Fred and too late to save themselves.

The henchmen shrugged again, their shoulders rising and falling in perfect unison. "You'll have to ask the master. He knows *everything*. Speaking of the master," they added with matching shudders, "we'd better get you up there. He doesn't like to be kept waiting."

Oh yes, time was definitely running out.

Fast.

"What about Fred? I need to see her. I need to know she's alright. *Please*," Emba begged.

The henchmen shook their heads. "The master said to bring you straight up to him. He's got his cauldron all ready for you."

A cauldron? Emba was the one shuddering now. How much blood would Necromalcolm need to fill one of those?

"Come on," ordered Odolf's henchman. "Less talking…"

"…And more walking," finished his double. "Up we go now."

All four staircases looked identical. Maybe they were. Maybe there was one for each identical henchman. Maybe that's why Emba found herself shoved towards one, while Odolf was dragged towards another. She could see him out of the corner of her eye though, as they began the long climb, edging out of sight as she rounded the first bend, only to reappear again as the staircases crossed further up.

"It's going to be alright," he whispered as they passed each other again, shooting her his best 'brave warrior' smile.

"Yes," agreed Emba, wishing she believed him. Wishing for the hundredth time that she hadn't lost her pouch that fateful day, and shown Necromalcolm where to find her. Wishing for a dragon to swoop down through the red crack in the sky and carry her away from the cauldron-shaped doom that was waiting for her at the top. Carry them *all* away—her, Odolf and Fred. But when she looked up now, all she saw was the never-ending twist of staircases above her, spiralling in and out of each other like stone snakes.

Up and up they climbed, past heavy, dragon-carved doors built into the curving wall. Round and round and round, until Emba's head grew woozy and her vision began to swim.

Don't look down, she told herself. Too late—she already had.

Woah! How did the ground get so far away?

"Steady now," said the henchman, steering her back onto course as she swayed perilously close to the edge. "The master wants you in one piece."

Only so he can drain my blood, thought Emba bitterly, dragging her eyes back from the sickening drop below to the staircase ahead of her. One step at a time. Then another. And another. *And then what?* she thought. *Once he's taken all my blood for his cauldron, what then?* She imagined dark, shadowy hands helping her over the parapet at the top of the tower... helping her to her final, free-falling fate. That's if she was still alive by the time Necromalcolm had finished with her. Or maybe he'd get one of his eerily identical henchmen to do his dirty work for him. Yes, she could imagine that all too easily. She could imagine those same strong hands that she could feel at her back now, lifting her up like a spent sack of flour and tossing her to her doom. She could imagine the screaming rush of air against her face as she plummeted towards the waiting ground below. And the terrible *crack* as she... no, no, no, she didn't want to imagine *that*.

Such violent, ground-splatting thoughts did little to help the wooziness in Emba's head as they circled up further and further. Odolf was little more than a giddying smudge of colour and movement when they passed each other now. A dizzy blur. Emba found herself longing to reach the top—longing for the endless climb to be over—even as she dreaded what she'd find waiting for her there. *Who* she'd find waiting for her…

And then, just when she thought she couldn't climb another step, the last dragon-carved door finally swam into view. There was nothing above them now but the stone roof of the tower.

"Here we go," said the henchman cheerfully, as if he was leading her to a merry feast rather than her doom. "I'll let the master know we're here." He leaned past her and rapped on the carved door with his big, hairy knuckles.

"At last," called a deep, echoing voice that sent sparking jolts of recognition through every vein in Emba's body. "I've been expecting you."

Chapter 22

The Appalling Announcement of Terrible Truth

Emba stepped out onto the top of the tower, and there he was—Necromalcolm. He was tall and thin-faced, like the duchess, with high cheekbones, glittering eyes and flowing grey-flecked hair that whipped around his head in the gusting wind. In many ways he was exactly like Emba had imagined him; with an impressively long beard, and heavy robes stretching all the way down to the floor. There were no snakes nesting in his beard though, she was relieved to see. No moths, or bugs or ancient crumbs of half-chewed food. So much for her unwashed theory. Whatever it was that upset the duchess when she saw her brother, it wasn't a lack of personal hygiene. Even his fingernails looked clean, as he held out his arms to her.

"My darling!" he called. "You don't know how long I've waited for this moment. Come to Daddy."

Emba stared at him in surprise. No, not in surprise—in shock. In confusion. In jaw-dropping, eye-popping disbelief. What did he mean? Surely he wasn't talking to *her?* She turned round to see Odolf emerging through the roof door behind her—how was that even possible? How did all the staircases lead to the same door?—with his henchman in tow. But Odolf's father had died of the Sweating Plague, and the henchman looked far too old and beardy to be Necromalcolm's son. Which only left one explanation... Necromalcolm must be mad. Yes, she thought, ignoring the strange tingling feeling in her veins. His magic must have turned his mind. That was the only thing that made any sense. Because *he* certainly wasn't making any.

There was the cauldron, just like the henchman had said—an enormous metal beast of a pot, big enough to cook an entire cow in. Emba could see something thick and slimy-looking inside, hissing and fizzing to itself as it bubbled away, waiting for her blood. But Necromalcolm seemed more interested in *hugging* her than cutting open her veins.

"My little dragon girl," he said. "Look at you now! The last time I saw you, you were just an egg."

"I er…" Emba didn't know what to say. She didn't know what to think. On the one hand, the fact that he hadn't already sliced her open with a knife—or a spell—was a good thing. A *very* good thing. But on the other hand, this was getting seriously strange.

"*Your* dragon girl?" repeated Odolf. "You saw her when she was still an egg?"

"Yes," said Necromalcolm. His eyes weren't just glittering now, they were blazing. "Right before her dragon mother stole her away."

My mother? Emba's throat tightened and her head throbbed. It was all she could do to remember to breathe. *My mother was a dragon.* Hearing it from Necromalcolm's lips as a cold, hard fact made it feel more real, somehow. Real and wrong and more confusing than ever… because her mother was only half of the story, wasn't she?

"And my father?" Emba murmured, knowing what he was going to say. He'd *already* said it. *Come to*

Daddy... My little dragon girl.

"*I'm* your father," he said, scowling back at her. "It was my blood—mine and the dragon's—that went into that spell. My blood that made you."

"Why?" she asked. *Why did you make the egg in the first place? Why did my mother steal me away then abandon me in the woods?*

"Why?" he repeated. "To harness the power of flight, of course. To have dominion over the skies and seize control over this realm and theirs. And for that I needed dragon blood..." He stared up at the clouds. Could *he* see the red crack pulsing overhead? "There was a time, hundreds of years ago, when dragons roamed the earth freely, before the breach between their realm and ours was sealed. Before they were relegated to stories and myths. To legends. But the old spells told of a way to break that seal. They told of a charm to steal the dragon's power and give wings to the wingless. To make a man fly and crown him ruler of all the earth and heavens."

Emba found herself staring up at the sky too, picturing another world beyond theirs. A world of wonder and strange marvels. A world of dragons. Could the breach be opening again? Is that what the red crack meant? And the flaming feeling in her belly?

"It would take a magician of untold power and brilliance to tear open the seal—to summon forth a living, breathing dragon," said Necromalcolm, pulling back his shoulders and puffing out his chest. His face took on a strange, eerie glow. "It would take a magician of immeasurable strength and cunning to *hold* a dragon long enough to steal its blood. But I was the most powerful necromancer in the land, with legions of the dead at my command. If anyone could decipher the ancient spells and cast them correctly, it was me. I'd already broken the veil between Life and Death, summoning up the spirits of the departed to do my bidding, so why couldn't I break the veil between this world and the dragons' world too?" There was a darker, more menacing edge to his voice now. "And that's exactly what I did. I ripped open that breach like I was tearing through silk, draining the blood from that fearsome beast like a maid milking a cow. I was unstoppable. I was invincible…" He stretched out his arms again—to the heavens, this time—as if he was reliving his own glory.

"And then?" asked Emba.

"And then?" echoed Odolf.

"And then..." Necromalcolm's arms dropped back to his sides and he shook his head. "And then I mixed it with my blood, just like the ancient spell said, and I intoned the ancient words of transformation... and then..."

He closed his eyes and threw back his head and howled a terrible howl that seemed to shake the sky, setting the tower trembling beneath Emba's feet. Or maybe *she* was the one trembling. Trembling with wonder and terror and dread at what was coming. But she had to know... she had to know what happened.

"And then?" she asked again.

"And then I got the hiccups," said Necromalcolm, turning on her with a vicious snarl, as if it was all her fault. "And the spell backfired. Maybe the words didn't come out quite right—because of the hiccups, I mean, not because I didn't know how to say them—or maybe it was because I'd taken the dragon's blood by force… but something went wrong, and instead of the power of the skies and dominion over all, I ended up with an egg instead. An egg that was stolen from under my nose," he said, the words curdling with anger, "while I was rooted to the spot, powerless to stop it. I should have killed that pesky dragon while I had the chance. I should have finished it off for good."

I'm glad you didn't, thought Emba. *I'm glad the dragon got away. My mother…*

My girl, my girl, my girl, the invisible beat of wings sounded above her head.

"But if you're as powerful as all that, why can't you open the breach again and find *another* dragon?" asked Odolf. "Why do you need Emba?"

"Ah yes," said Necromalcolm, as if he was noticing Odolf properly for the first time. "My sister told me all about you in her message. The *famous* belt-buckle thief." His voice was low and venomous. "Do you know how long it took me to summon up the magic for that buckle? Magic that was meant to protect me when I finally found my missing daughter and cast my dragon-blood spell again. It looks like I'll have to manage without it though, doesn't it, thanks to *you*. But then again, it's thanks to you that I found my daughter, so I suppose I should be grateful for that. If you hadn't told my henchman where to find her, we wouldn't be here now, would we?"

Odolf's cheeks flushed. "I didn't know who he was," he said, defensively. "I didn't know who *you* were either. You say you're the most powerful necromancer in the land, but I'd never even heard of you."

"I said I *was* the most powerful necromancer in the land," roared Necromalcolm. "Until that spell backfired, making me a prisoner in my own tower. Instead of giving me the skies, it rooted me to the earth." He lifted up his robes as he spoke and Odolf gasped in horror.

Emba didn't just gasp, she cried out loud: "Ugh, yuck!"

Necromalcolm's legs were like tree trunks, with roots instead of feet, reaching down into the stone floor beneath him, anchoring him in place. Emba found herself thinking of the snare trees in Witchingford Wood, squeezing at their captives' flesh with their powerful, gnarled tendrils.

"I've tried everything I can to reverse it," he said, "believe me. But the spell's too strong. It took most of my powers along with my legs. How am I supposed to conquer the dragon realm like *this?*" he hissed. "Even the dead have deserted me."

"So that's why you didn't come to find me," Emba said. "You *couldn't*. That's why you needed your scrying bowl. And that's why you had to lure me here instead, by taking Fred."

Necromalcolm scowled, letting his robes fall back down over his roots. "Yes," he said. "All those years of searching and then finally, *finally*, I caught a glimpse of you in the woods. I saw the scales on your arms and legs, and the yellow of your eyes, and I knew you were the child I'd been looking for. The fact that you were playing in a hog chestnut tree at the time—a rare, distinctive tree as I'm sure you know—was a stroke of fortune. *That's* how I found you. With a little help from your friend here," he said, gesturing to Odolf. "The boy told my henchman how close you were to the old crone who'd taken you in. How she was like a mother to you. I wasn't sure you'd come if I told you the truth—if I simply asked nicely. But I knew if I took *her*, you'd follow of your own accord. And here you are."

"I'm sorry," Odolf whispered. "I meant it in a *good* way—about Fred, I mean. Not in a why-don't-you-try-kidnapping-her sort of way. And I never called her a crone, I swear. I *wouldn't*. I love her too, you know."

"But I still don't understand," said Emba. For a moment there it had all made sense, but the more she thought about it the more confusing it got. "Fred said I'd be safe in the cave—that's what the lullaby was for—but once you'd got me away from there, I was defenceless. You could have ordered your henchmen to get my blood for you. Why did you need to drag me all the way out here?"

"Because you're my daughter. I wanted to meet you. And because I couldn't risk the spell going wrong a second time. I still don't know if it was the hiccups that made it backfire before, or because I took the dragon's blood by force. That's why I need you to give me *your* blood willingly. Like the kind, dutiful daughter I know you are… The kind of daughter I'd be proud to call my heir."

But I don't want to be your *daughter*, thought Emba. *Fred's the only parent I've ever needed.*

"Please," Necromalcolm begged, changing tack. "I just want my legs back, that's all. No more dreams of flying—I've learned my lesson there. No more taking over the world with my magic. I just want to be a normal person again. That's not too much to ask is it?" His dark eyes glinted.

Really? Emba wanted to believe him. She wanted to believe that there was a nice, neat, happy ending for them all lurking within her reach. But could she trust him? Was it really possible for a wicked sorcerer like him to change his ways?

Necromalcolm touched his finger to her wrist shackles and they fell away like dry autumn leaves. Then he reached into his robes and pulled out a jewelled goblet and a short, gleaming knife. "One cup ought to do it," he said, with a thin-lipped smile. "One little cup for Daddy, there's a good girl."

Chapter 23

The Blade and the Blood
(and the Gnarly Old Knees)

Emba could hear dragon wings beating overhead again. *Beware*, they seemed to say now, just like they had in the woods. *Beware, beware, beware*. She stared at the blood-catching goblet and the glittering blade, and shook her head. "No," she said.

Necromalcolm's smile melted away. "No?" he repeated. "*No?* That's not very *daughterly* of you," he hissed.

"Well it's not very fatherly of you to ask," replied Emba. He wasn't interested in *her* at all, was he? Only in her blood. And he wasn't interested in changing his ways either. Of course he wasn't. "I'm not giving you anything until I see Fred," she told him, with as much firmness as she could muster. "Not until you let her go. And Odolf too."

"And that's it?" he asked. "If I release them, you'll do as I ask?" His eyes narrowed. "But how do I know you'll keep your word?" He slipped the goblet back into his robe and held out the knife on its own. "How about one tiny little drop now, as a sign of your promise, and *then* I'll release them. You can give me the rest once you know they're safe."

Beware, beware, beware.

"Don't do it," hissed Odolf. "You can't trust him."

No, agreed Emba, silently. *I can't.* But what choice did she have? She'd come all this way to save Fred— there was no turning back now. One drop of blood to save her beloved guardian, and her trusted friend who'd risked everything to help her, seemed like a small price to pay. A single drop, that was all. How much harm could it do?

She took hold of the knife and walked over to the cauldron, ignoring the trembling in her legs. The green mixture smelt of serpentweed and dried fish, and something sharp and metallic that Emba couldn't quite place. It fizzed and spat as she held her shaking hand over the top, touching the sharp point of the knife to the soft pad of her finger and pressing down.

Time seemed to slow as a single bead of blood bubbled up through her skin. As it dropped towards the waiting cauldron like a rich red jewel. Emba watched it falling... falling... fall—

HISSSSSSSS!

The mixture frothed and foamed as Emba's blood landed. It boiled and churned. She wrenched her hand away, stumbling backwards in fright. What was happening? What had she done? But even as she pulled back, Necromalcolm was already lunging forwards, reaching his own hands over the fiercely churning mixture and chanting under his breath. The words were soft and snakelike: strange slippery sounds that Emba could barely hear, let alone understand. But something was happening to the mixture as he whispered them. It was settling now, the wild spitting growing tamer and calmer, the furious fizzing easing to a gentle simmer.

Necromalcolm retrieved the jewelled goblet and dipped it into the cauldron, scooping up a full cup of frothing green gloop. Emba stared in disbelief.

He wasn't going to *drink* it was he?

Yes. He certainly was.

Necromalcolm tilted back his head as he brought the goblet to his lips, tipping the mixture down his throat in one big, gurgling gulp.

"Ah," he cried with a sigh of satisfaction, wiping green slime from his mouth.

"AHHHHHHHH!" His eyebrows shot upwards. "AAHHHOWWWWWW!" The whites of his eyes turned red and his mouth began to foam, as a wild juddering took hold of his body.

"What's happening?" asked Odolf.

"I don't know," said Emba, watching in horror as Necromalcolm's head whipped from one side to the other with such violence she thought it might fly off altogether. And yet she couldn't tear her eyes away. Shadowy faces swirled around him, with hollow eyes and wide screaming mouths. Perhaps they were his spirits, Emba thought, the idea sending fresh shivers through her body. The spirits of the dead coming back to their master.

Necromalcolm raised up his arms and his robes

lifted up too, as if they were being drawn on invisible strings. And his roots… they were lifting as well, pulling themselves up out of the stone floor with a sucking, squelching sound. Pulling themselves out and wriggling free, snaking off across the tower like living creatures.

"BEHOLD!" roared Necromalcolm as the bark on his tree legs fell away to reveal bare white bones beneath. But even as Emba watched, the bones oozed out muscles and tendons, and flesh and blood and skin. They grew feet and toes and thick woollen socks in a fetching shade of pink. And then boots—long black boots with silver dragon buckles.

His head grew still and the reds of his eyes turned white—their dark centres glittering with triumph. The juddering in his body eased to a gentle shiver as he lowered his arms, and his robes sank back to the floor. The shadowy shapes stopped their silent screaming, melting away into nothingness. It looked like it was all over, whatever 'it' was.

"Yes!" cried Necromalcolm, wiping green foam from his lips. "It worked! I'm free!"

Emba took another step back. "I'm glad," she lied, thinking how much more dangerous he'd be now. He might be her father—sort of—but that didn't mean he wasn't an evil sorcerer who'd stop at nothing to get what he wanted. And if he'd already *got* what he wanted, where did that leave her? And Fred and Odolf? "Now that *you're* free," she told him, "you need to free my friends, like you promised."

Necromalcolm took no notice. "But will it be enough?" he murmured to himself, walking to the edge of the tower and climbing up onto the parapet. The wind whipped at his hair and robes, as he flung back his head to the sky and began flapping his arms like a demented chicken. So much for having given up on his dreams of flight.

"By the power of dragon blood, I rise to the skies," he roared. Nothing happened. Necromalcolm flapped harder. "I *said*, by the power of dragon blood, I rise to the skies!"

For one breath-holding moment Emba wondered what would happen if she were to creep up behind him and push. Would his magic be strong enough to stop his fall? Would his shadowy spirits pull him back out of danger? Or would he plummet to the ground below like a mere mortal? Like a man? But there was nothing in the prophecy about that. Nothing heroic about pushing someone to their death while their back was turned. No, she shook the thought away again. That wasn't how heroes in stories saved the day. And what about Fred? What if Emba needed her father's magic to set her guardian free?

"Curses," cried Necromalcolm, lowering his arms and clambering back off the parapet. "Not enough dragon blood," he said. "That's the problem."

"You'll get your blood when you free my friends," said Emba. "Let them go."

Necromalcolm's eyes narrowed. His fingers twitched. "No one talks to me like that," he hissed under his breath. "No one tells *me* what to do."

Emba gulped. "Please," she added. "That's what we agreed."

Necromalcolm stared at her. A long, hard stare, as if he was deciding what to do with her. "Very well," he agreed at last. "You," he said, clicking his fingers at Emba's henchman. "Fetch the old crone and bring her here."

"She's not an old crone," said Emba, feeling the heat rise in her throat. "She's wise and wonderful and more of a parent than you'll ever be."

"Fine," snarled Necromalcolm. "Fetch the wise and wonderful old woman and let's get this over with."

"Wait a minute. I'm not sure Fred will be able to manage all those stairs," said Emba. "Her knees aren't what they were. Perhaps we should join her down in the cellar instead." She was thinking of the prophecy again, of the 'safety' in those 'walls of stone', where Fred lay 'weeping in the deep'. The Tome of Terrible Tomorrows hadn't mentioned anything about towers and sky. It hadn't mentioned the sudden wind screaming round her cheeks or the fearsome drop on the other side of the parapet. Yes, that drop. Emba was thinking of that again too… of how easy it would be for Necromalcolm to blast them over the side once he'd got what he wanted. And then of course there were Fred's knees to think about as well. She really *would* struggle to get up all those hundreds of stairs.

Necromalcolm sighed. "Alright, fine. Stand back." He cracked his knuckles and pointed at the cauldron, muttering a fresh spell under his breath. The cauldron floated upwards, as if it was weightless, drifting over to the magically open door on the shoulders of dark shadowy shapes. His spirits were back again.

Emba shivered at the darkness of her father's magic. There was a slightly less magical moment when the cauldron got stuck halfway, wedged in tight against the too-small doorway, but another whisper from Necromalcolm brought more dark shadows to stretch the doorframe wider, allowing the cauldron to sail on through.

"Hurry up," he snapped, motioning to the henchmen to follow with the prisoners. "The sooner we get down there, the sooner I can take power over the skies... and then *all* the worlds will bow down before my might and majesty!"

"What does he mean by that?" whispered Odolf as they reached the tower door.

"I dread to think," said Emba. "I guess we'll find out soon enough."

Chapter 24

The Calamitous Climax

"Oh Emba dear, of *course* I'm glad to see you," said Fred, wiping her tears on the back of her gnarly old hand. Her left eye was twitching furiously. "And you too, Odolf. But you shouldn't be here. You shouldn't have come. You should have stayed in the cave where you were safe."

After their dizzying descent, climbing all the way back down the tower, and then down a second, secret staircase hidden beneath the metal cover in the mosaic floor, all Emba had wanted was for Fred to hold her in her arms and tell her everything was going to be alright. But the old lady had taken one look at her and Odolf, and the cauldron floating down beside them, and started sobbing. It wasn't quite the welcome

Emba had hoped for. At least Fred was still in one piece though. At least she was still alive. Whatever *calamitous* fate Necromalcolm had in mind for her, he hadn't unleashed it yet.

"How could we stay home and do nothing, knowing you were in danger?" Emba protested. "Knowing they'd already hurt you. We saw the blood on the cave floor." Her eyes were busy scanning the old lady for signs of injury even as she spoke, but there were no obvious gaping wounds, thank goodness.

"Blood?" repeated Fred with a frown. "The men who took me weren't exactly *nice*," she said, narrowing her eyes at the nearest henchman. "There's nothing nice about sticking a sack over an old lady's head and carting her off in the middle of the night. But they didn't hurt me. Are you sure it wasn't nightberry juice? I was in such a state with that business over the dragon and Necromalcolm I forgot to drink it before I went to bed. Perhaps they knocked it over while they were dragging me out the cave."

Emba didn't know whether to laugh or cry. For days now, she'd been picturing Fred lying on the cave floor wounded and in pain... and it was nightberry juice all along.

"But even if it *was* blood," said Fred, "you still shouldn't have come after me. You should have stayed at home where it was safe, and let me worry about how I'm going to get out of this. As for giving that man *your* precious blood, don't even think about it."

"It's too late," said Emba, bravely. "I gave him my word. If that's what it takes to save you, then that's what I'm going to do."

"You heard her," snarled Necromalcolm. "Now shut up, you old crone, and let her get on with it."

"No. Don't do it, Emba," Fred begged, her left eye on twitching overdrive. "Don't listen to him... I've had a good life. If this is the end for me then so be it. I'd rather meet my death with dignity than let you suffer at his hands. And once he's got power over the skies, there'll be no stopping him..."

"ENOUGH!" roared Necromalcolm. The cellar walls trembled. "No more talking." He pointed his finger at Odolf and his shackles shook themselves off his wrists, falling away in pieces. Then he did the same to the chains round Fred's ankles. "There, your friends are free, just like I promised. Now let the blood-draining begin." He held out the knife and goblet to Emba for a second time.

Emba shook her head, stubbornly. "*Properly* free, I meant, not stuck down in a cellar surrounded by henchmen. Let them go home."

"I'm not going anywhere," said Fred, equally stubbornly. "Not without you."

"And nor am I," agreed Odolf.

"ENOUGH, I SAID!" Necromalcolm roared, throwing down the goblet in rage. He grabbed hold of Emba's wrist and dragged her over to the cauldron. "No more games, girl. Give me your blood or your friends die, got it?"

"Alright," Emba whimpered. "Don't hurt them."

"But it's got to be willingly given," hissed Necromalcolm, his face twisted with impatience. "I can't risk anything going wrong this time. You have to *want* me to take it."

"I do. I want you to have it. Here," said Emba, reaching for her toenail pouch and yanking if off over her head. "I've even taken off my protective charm. There's nothing stopping you now. Please, take whatever you need."

She shut her eyes as Necromalcolm held her hand over the simmering green mixture. *Please don't let it hurt. Please let it be quick.* She held her breath as he brought the knife's blade to her waiting palm. And then, as the knife cut into her flesh, Emba Oak stopped holding her breath and started crying instead. She could already feel the blood trickling out of the cut as the pain bit.

"Noooo!" came Odolf's voice from behind. Emba opened her eyes to see him launching himself at Necromalcolm, trying to wrestle the knife from his clutches. But a single whisper from the sorcerer sent Odolf flying backwards through the air, smacking into the cellar wall with a sickening thump.

He didn't get up again.

He didn't move.

Emba wrenched her hand from Necromalcolm's grasp, blood still trickling out of the cut, and rushed to her friend's side. Her stomach twisted in fear. Hot, raw fear, tinged with anger. "Odolf, are you alright? Say something, please."

But Odolf lay still and quiet.

"Come back," shouted Necromalcolm, chasing after her. "You're spilling your precious blood on the floor. You're wasting it."

"Odolf?" Drops of blood and tears fell onto his cheeks as Emba leaned over him. "Please, Odolf, wake up." Her stomach burned hotter and hotter at the sight of his pale, lifeless face, a wild, burning rage rising in her chest. *No, no, no, no, no. This wasn't how his hero story was supposed to end.*

"Leave him and get back to the cauldron," commanded the necromancer, seizing her by the shoulder. "Or the old crone will be next."

Emba whipped round to face her father, her whole body alight with anger. A burning heat sizzled through her veins, flickering up her legs and arms and crackling in her belly. "What have you done?" she hissed.

"Y-your eyes," stammered Necromalcolm, taking a step back. "You've got the dragon eyes! Look at them! Oh yes!"

Emba barely heard him. "What have you done to Odolf?" she demanded, smoke trailing from her mouth and nose as she pulled herself back onto her feet, her gaze still fixed on Necromalcolm.

"Dragon's breath," he cried. "You've got the dragon's breath! How does it feel?"

But Emba couldn't have answered him if she wanted. She was nothing *but* anger now. "You killed him!" Red-hot fury came tearing up from her belly as she roared with rage. "You killed my friend!"

Her throat was a burning tunnel of heat. A rush of flame shot out of her mouth and blasted across the cellar like a beam of light.

Necromalcolm staggered backwards, his beard and hair on fire.

"Dragon's blaze," he cried, slapping at his burning beard with his hands and setting light to his sleeves in the process. "You've got the dragon's blaze." His voice crackled like the flames dancing round his face, as he stumbled back towards the waiting cauldron.

"Look out!" cried Emba, watching through the clouding smoke as he teetered and tipped, the burning hatred of her anger already beginning to cool. Or maybe she only *thought* it: *Look out!* Maybe her throat was still too hot and raw for words. But it was too late, either way.

There was a muffled clunk, a cry, a wild flailing of fiery arms... and then a splash.

Emba would never forget that splash. Would never forget the look on Necromalcolm's face as he toppled back into the bubbling pot, his mouth stretched wide in a silent scream, his dark eyes bulging.

One moment he was there, and the next moment he was gone. It felt like forever to Emba, watching on in horror, but that's all it was—one single moment that changed everything.

The cauldron bubbled and gushed, a mighty column of foaming green gloop cascading up towards the ceiling and then falling back down with a screaming hiss.

"Master!" called the henchmen in unison, rushing to the cauldron and staring down into its bubbling depths. But if they were waiting for their master to rise back out of the green gloop and command them to help him, they must have been disappointed. There were no more commands to be issued. There was no more Necromalcolm.

Emba swayed on the spot, clutching at her bleeding palm. She felt light-headed and dizzy, scarcely able to take in what had happened. Odolf... The flames... Necromalcolm...

And then Fred was there, wrapping Emba in her arms to keep her from falling. Hot tears sizzled and steamed down Emba's cheeks as Fred called for the bewildered henchmen to fetch fresh comfic and threadbalm leaves from Necromalcolm's herb garden.

Emba let out a hoarse, painful cry of grief as the full enormity of what had happened struck home, then collapsed, sobbing, into the warmth of her guardian's chest. "Odolf, oh Odolf." She was dimly aware of Fred stroking her hair and telling her it was going to be alright but Emba knew that nothing would ever be alright again.

"Shh, he's going to be alright," Fred said a second time.

Wait a minute, thought Emba, struggling to make

sense of what she was hearing. She could have sworn Fred said that *he* was going to be alright. But how could he? Odolf was dead.

"He's just a bit winded, that's all," added Fred. "It'd take more than an evil necromancer to defeat a fearless hero like you, wouldn't it Odolf?"

"Odolf Bravebuckle at your service," came the slightly shaky reply.

Odolf!

Emba tore herself free from Fred's arms and raced over to her friend. He was pale—horribly pale—but his eyes were open and he was grinning.

"I guess necromancers are like bears," he said, raising his eyebrow. "It's best to play dead when they attack. Unless you're an amazing fire-breathing dragon girl, that is."

Chapter 25

The Happily ~~Ever After~~ for a Bit Ending

All the best stories end in triumph and feasting, with evil vanquished and all the loose ends neatly tied up. Yes, Emba Oak had listened to enough entertaining tales round the fire to know that a story wouldn't be a proper story without a celebratory feast and a well-earned happily ever after at the end… and hers, it would seem, was no exception. Well, except for the feasting part. Emba wasn't sure wild mushrooms and a stale loaf of bread from Necromalcolm's kitchen counted as a feast, but it was good enough.

He's really gone, she told herself as she sat outside the tower with Fred and Odolf, finishing off the last of their makeshift meal. Her throat was painfully sore and her hand stung beneath its comfic and threadbalm bandage, but Emba was too tired—and too relieved—to care. The evil father she never even knew she had was gone, and she was finally safe. As for her mother... For a moment Emba thought she heard something—a soft beating of wings above her head, *he's gone, he's gone, he's gone*, or was it *you're mine, you're mine, you're mine?*—but when she looked up at the sky, the red crack had disappeared.

That's good, Emba told herself, ignoring the peculiar pang of disappointment in her chest. *That's how it should be. Dragons should stay in their world where they belong, and humans should stay in theirs. And as for half-dragon, half-human girls, they should... they should stop worrying about things they can't change and be grateful for friends who love them just as they are. Yes. Exactly.*

She turned back to her friends with a smile. Odolf and Fred were still deciphering the prophecy that the Tome had shown Emba. "So the safety in walls of stone bit was about us," said Odolf. The colour had returned to his cheeks now, and he seemed back to his normal self. "It was telling us to stay in the cave."

Fred nodded. "Not that you listened," she replied with a fond grin.

"And you were the stolen heart and broken art that was weeping in the deep?"

"Yes, that was me," said Fred. "My magic was well and truly broken. I couldn't get the simplest of charms to work within the tower walls. Necromalcolm's power was too strong, even in his reduced state."

"And the tongues of pain and fire must have been Emba," said Odolf, "seeking your freedom. But Necromalcolm was the one shaking shackles and breaking bonds, so doesn't that make *him* the hero? That's what the prophecy said, *bonds shall break and shackles shake before the hero's ire*."

"Sometimes words can be read more than one way," Fred explained. "It could mean that the bonds will break *in the force* of the hero's ire, or it could simply mean that they'll break *first*, before the hero unleashes her ire."

"But what is 'ire'?" Emba cut in.

"It's another word for anger," said Fred. "For rage. And you certainly had plenty of that. It was your *ire* that awakened the flames inside you."

"Oh," said Emba. "I thought it was short for 'iron'."

"Me too," said Odolf. "I thought it might be my belt buckle, which would mean *I* was the hero in the prophecy. But then when the thieves stole it, I knew it wasn't me after all."

"You seemed pretty heroic to me," Fred told him, "tackling Necromalcolm like that."

And what about 'calamitous'? thought Emba. *What does that mean?* But the conversation had already moved on.

"What do you think happened to him?" Odolf asked. "I had a stir around inside the cauldron while you were sorting out Emba's wound and there was no sign of his body. It's like he boiled clean away."

"I don't know," said Fred. "Perhaps he got the mixture wrong. Or perhaps it was Emba's blood—he said it wouldn't work if he took it by force but that's exactly what he did. He forced her to give it to him, in order to save us."

"Or perhaps it wasn't strong enough to give him full dragon powers, after all," said Odolf. "Only lizard ones. Perhaps he turned into a lizard and ran away."

Fred laughed. "Lizard powers? You are funny, Odolf," she said. "I don't think so, thank goodness. I don't like the thought of Necromalcolm running *anywhere*. I guess we'll never know for sure what happened. All that matters is he's gone now, and he won't be bothering us anymore."

But it wasn't only Necromalcolm taking *her* blood, Emba realised with a start. She had *his* blood too. *It was his blood that made me.* She felt queasy, just thinking about it. If her dragon blood had given her scales and fire, what might her wicked sorcerer's blood unleash in her? "I won't end up like him, will I?" she asked. "Evil, I mean. Not boiled away in a cauldron," she added, although she didn't fancy that very much either. "I mean, he *was* my father."

"Of course not, Emba dear." Fred reached for her hand and squeezed it tight. "You're pure goodness, through and through. You both are," she said, reaching for Odolf's hand too.

The compliment was wasted on Odolf though. *He* was looking a little queasy as well.

"Supposing I *did* spot something like a lizard near the cauldron, scuttling away into the shadows," he said. "A sort of strange, wizardy-looking lizard. What then?"

"I don't know," Fred told him. "I guess you'd catch hold of it, just in case. Take it somewhere far, far away where it couldn't hurt anyone."

"Ah," said Odolf, the colour draining back out of his cheeks. "Oh dear. I think it might be a little late for that."

The End

Join Emba's next adventure in...

EMBA
OAK

AND THE

BECKONING
BONES

Want to read more by Jenny Moore?

AGENT STARLING: OPERATION BAKED BEANS

Baked beans might seem harmless but, in the wrong hands and the wrong millennium, they can do a surprising amount of damage.

11-year-old Oliver Starling thinks Romans are ancient history... until he teams up with Agent Owl to stop an evil mastermind, Dr Midnight, from conquering Roman Britain with baked beans and nappy pins. Armed with only a photo booth time machine and a pocket history guide, can Oliver and Owl keep Dr Midnight from changing the course of history forever?

AUDREY ORR and the ROBOT RAGE

Ever wished there was more than one of you to go round? Need to be in two places at once?

When Audrey Orr's mum wins a luxury cruise to Norway, Audrey thinks she's won the jackpot—until she realises it's during term-time. With her no-nonsense headteacher, Mr Stickler, on her case, she has to resort to something a bit unusual: a robot clone! But can she trust Awesome the clone to stay home and pretend to be her or will Awesome turn out to be a bit... Awful?

Bauble, Me and the Family Tree

Noel is used to his unusual family set-up: him, Mum, super-brainy little sister Bauble, and his gay uncles (both called Mike) next door. But when Bauble spots Mum kissing Santa Claus—in August— everything Noel thought he knew about his family is turned upside-down.

Who's the mysterious 'F' sending Mum romantic postcards? Why has she started taking weird photos of people in food bikinis? And, even though he's clearly not Santa, might Dad still be alive after all?

The MISADVENTURES of NICHOLAS NABB

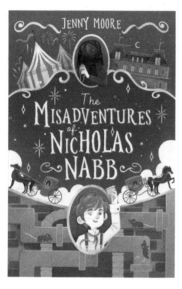

I was a goner and I knew it. Everyone knew it. Only that's when the lady in the black veil appeared.

A botched bread roll robbery spells trouble for Victorian sewer scamp, Nicholas Nabb— big trouble. But when a mysterious veiled widow, Annie, steps in to save him, it looks like his luck might finally be changing. Only Annie vanishes before they can become properly acquainted, leaving Nick with nothing but questions.

Who is the lady behind the black veil? Why does she seem determined to help him? And, most importantly of all, where is she now? Nick will stop at nothing to find out.